Runway Rumors

Hey Friend,

Guess what? We got invited to New York City to compete in a big fashion show. We've never modeled before so we can't wait to see what it's like!

Grab your best outfit and come rock the runway with us! But watch out, because who knows what trouble we'll find once we get there.

Love you!
The Sister Detectives

GISELLE   EVANGELINE   MERCEDES

GEM Sisters®

Hang Out With GEM Sisters

Join the club!
www.gemsisters.com

Watch on YouTube

/gemsisters

GEM MAIL

Write to us!
GEM Sisters
P.O. Box 3062
Glendale, CA 91221

Fashion Trouble!

"Look!" whispered Giselle. "Someone's in there with a flashlight. I can see a bunch of clothing racks."

"I want to see. Turn the phone," ordered Mercedes on the phone screen.

"Hold on. We'll call you back," said Evangeline as she ended the video call.

Evangeline and Giselle snuck inside the room together. They crawled on the floor trying to hide in the darkness.

BUZZ! BUZZ! BUZZ!

The stranger quickly turned at the sound.

Evangeline pressed the button to end the call. It was too late. She ducked down and crawled under a clothing rack.

Giselle could see Evangeline was in danger. The person with the flashlight crept closer to where her sister was hiding.

Evangeline was so scared she could hear her own heartbeat.

Sneakily, Giselle sent a text message then powered down her phone.

Back in the lobby Mercedes phone beeped a text message alert. There was only one word on screen . . . *HELP*!

Sister Detectives

Runway Rumors

By MéLisa Lomelino
& Ryun Hovind

MéLisa and Ryun Productions
Los Angeles, CA

For Joquena.
Our best friend and partner in crime
since the beginning.

ISBN-13: 978-1-947775-04-6
ISBN-10: 1947775046
ISBN-13 eBook: 978-1-947775-05-3

First Printing: May 2020
Manufactured in the United States of America.
MéLisa and Ryun Productions
6444 San Fernando Road #3062
Glendale, CA 91201

To see GEM Sisters' videos visit: youtube.com/gemsisters
To see behind the scenes of GEM Sisters check out their website: GEMSisters.com

Contents

CHAPTER 1

"Help me!" came a scream from the hotel bathroom.

Giselle and Evangeline ran over. The door was locked. They banged on it wildly.

"What's going on? Open up!" they both shouted.

Evangeline tucked in her shoulder and motioned for Giselle to move. She was going to break down the door. Giselle shook her head no. That was not a good idea.

Suddenly, they heard a small click and the door swung open. Their sister Mercedes stared angrily in the mirror. She was wearing a pink bathrobe with matching slippers.

Everything seemed to be okay. Evangeline looked for clues to understand what was wrong. She scanned the room for creepy spiders. Nothing.

"What's the deal drama queen?" asked Giselle, annoyed.

"I don't know what to wear!" replied Mercedes, holding up two outfits. "Duh!"

In one hand Mercedes held a hot pink glitter dress, and in the other a sparkly light pink dress.

"Those dresses look exactly the same! Girl, you need help," muttered Giselle as she walked out, disgusted.

Mercedes was happy to see Evangeline was still listening. "They're both fabulous. And I look amazing in each one of them. How can I possibly choose?"

Evangeline replied, "Okay try this out. Close your eyes . . ."

Mercedes shut her eyes and listened.

"Take a deep breath. Now throw them both in the air. Whichever one you catch is the one you wear!" exclaimed Evangeline.

Mercedes opened her eyes and glared. This was not the answer she wanted. She groaned and went back into the bathroom.

SLAM!

GEM Sisters were three real life sisters who were famous for making funny videos together. They each had beautiful brown skin and dark brown hair. The GEM name came from the first letter of the sisters' names: Giselle, Evangeline, and Mercedes.

Giselle was the oldest sister at 15. She liked to keep her hair short, dress in casual clothes, and wear lots of cute jewelry. She was supposed to be in charge of her little sisters, but they never listened.

Evangeline was the youngest sister at 10. She was known for her deep love of rainbows, unicorns, and always being silly. She collected odd things and was constantly trying out new hobbies.

Mercedes, at age 12, was the middle sister who always wanted attention. Her dream was to become famous and she would do anything to make it happen. She adored fashion and was known for her bold style.

GEM Sisters loved their fans and called them GEMS. Every day the sisters told their fans what they were doing on social media. Giselle went to the giant windows of their hotel room. She found the perfect lighting and started filming.

"Good morning GEMS! This weekend we're staying in New York City. We're like thirty floors up. Look at those skyscrapers out there.

Now, let's take a tour inside our messy hotel room! Dum dum DUM!"

It was a nice hotel room. Well at least it was until GEM Sisters slept there. The family had flown in the night before, and now the room looked like a disaster zone. Clothes were scattered everywhere as well as messy plates, used napkins, and open suitcases.

"Check this out," said Giselle, pointing to a room service food cart. "Here we have some half-eaten toast sitting on top of a wet moldy towel. I've got a mystery for you to solve. Which sister do you think made this mess?"

Talking about a mystery reminded Giselle of a secret she shared with her sisters. No one knew that together they solved cases as the Sister Detectives. They never went looking for cases to solve, but somehow mysteries always found them.

Giselle pointed the camera towards Evangeline. "Mystery solved! Here's the crumpled wet towel owner."

A focused Evangeline was drawing on the giant windows.

"What are you doing?" asked Giselle.

"It's art, darling," replied Evangeline in a silly French voice. "There's no explaining art.

Either you see it or you don't."

Evangeline was using different jellies and food items as art supplies. She had traced the New York City skyline on the window using grape jelly. Then she added emojis and monsters to the city scene. It looked like some sort of giant monster attack.

Giselle filmed Evangeline as she smashed a half-eaten bagel with cream cheese onto the window. She added raisins for eyes and bacon for legs.

"It's Bagel-Zilla! Oh no! Run for your lives!" shouted Evangeline.

She was drawing a helpless teenager getting mega-squished when strawberry jelly plopped onto her shirt.

"Oh no!" cried Giselle.

"Wait. Don't touch it!" warned Evangeline, grabbing her sketchbook.

Using her fork she dropped jelly blobs from her shirt onto the page. She drew a fancy dress with puffy sleeves.

"Voila!" exclaimed Evangeline. "My creation is born!"

Giselle looked confused and replied, "Um, your outfit is ruined. Aren't you gonna change?"

Evangeline reached into her giant suitcase

and pulled out a yellow fabric marker. She drew a circle around the jelly stain on her shirt. Then she decorated it into a heart eye emoji.

"Perfecto!" she exclaimed, "Now it's an Evangeline original."

Giselle spoke into the camera, "So, this is how Evangeline gets ready for our big fashion event. Today we're going to the headquarters for Totally Tiffany. I'm so excited!"

GEM Sisters had been invited to the world-famous fashion contest for the hottest tween clothing brand, Totally Tiffany. Every year the company's owner, Tiffany Vanguard, used the contest to choose one special girl to be the face of her clothing line.

Mercedes burst out of the bathroom. "I've decided on hot pink," she said, tossing the other dress on top of her suitcase.

Her sisters thought Mercedes was too nervous, while she felt they were too calm. For Mercedes this contest was serious. It was her big break to finally become . . . a model.

Mercedes slid into her new pink heels. She stepped in front of Giselle as she filmed.

"GEMS, when I win the contest I'll get my own bodyguard and I'll go on a world tour. Plus, I get to keep all the clothes in the collection!"

squealed Mercedes.

"All three of us were invited to compete," added Giselle. "Not just you, Mercedes."

Mercedes caught her reflection in the mirror and panicked. "This is all wrong. I should wear the light pink," she said, dashing back to the bathroom.

With her sisters gone, Giselle focused the camera back on her. She held up the book *Know New York in No Time*.

"I got this book at the airport. Did you know there are over eight million people who live in New York City? So I figure at least one of them has to be good boyfriend material. Right?"

Just then, Dad burst into the room, out of breath. "Why aren't you girls downstairs? All of the film gear is loaded into the taxi. Your mom is waiting with the driver. Every minute he waits is costing me a fortune!"

GEM Sisters' mom and dad owned a small video production studio back home in Los Angeles, California. They wanted to make big Hollywood movies, but instead they filmed whoever would hire them. Thanks to their daughters, this weekend they were filming a video about the Totally Tiffany fashion contest.

"Dad, I'm hungry!" complained Evangeline.

"What? You had room service," said Dad, frustrated as he pointed to the food cart.

"Well yeah, but that was art," said Evangeline, pointing to her outfit.

"Move it. Let's GO!" shouted Dad.

Mercedes came out of the bathroom now wearing the light pink dress. "Do you like my outfit, dad?"

"Sure," he quickly replied.

"That's the worst thing you could've said!" cried Mercedes as she ran back into the bathroom.

Poor Dad. With having three daughters, he could never say the right thing.

***

The taxi pulled up outside a brick building that was painted teal, pink, and white. A huge sign flashed "Totally Tiffany" in large neon letters. A long, welcome carpet led visitors inside.

An older smiling man in a blue suit greeted them and motioned to enter. "Hey there ladies, I'm Stan. Welcome to Totally Tiffany," he said in a thick Brooklyn accent.

"Bonjour, Doorman Stan," replied

Evangeline in her silly French voice.

"Bonjour, mademoiselle," Stan replied with a tip of his hat.

Once inside, the building was a dream come true. The large welcome lobby was full of bright colors and natural sunlight. The ceilings were so high they seemed to stretch on forever. Everything was polished and shiny.

The walls were covered with giant posters of beautiful models. Each year's winner was stunning in their Tiffany designs and fancy poses.

Dance music pumped through the speakers, making the whole room come alive. A beautiful blonde woman strutted toward them.

It was Tiffany! She had on the most eye-popping jewelry the girls had ever seen. She wore diamond earrings, fancy gold bracelets, and a sparkling, chunky necklace full of red rubies.

"Hi sweeties! It's the fabulous GEM Sisters!" exclaimed Tiffany.

She leaned in and gave each of the girls a kiss on both cheeks. The sisters thought it was strange, but they knew it was considered a fancy greeting and Tiffany was very fancy.

Tiffany observed their outfits and said,

"Mercedes, the hair, the shoes, the dress . . . love it, love it, love it! You are a walking doll."

"Oh this?" said Mercedes twirling in her hot pink dress. "It was just the first thing I put on this morning."

Giselle and Evangeline couldn't help but roll their eyes at Mercedes' lie.

Tiffany continued, "All of you look so fashionable. Remember ladies, you are only as beautiful as your outfit!"

"Sorry we're a little late," interrupted Dad. He instantly felt underdressed near this fashion icon with his blue jeans and faded plaid shirt. "You know how it is with girls and fashion."

"I don't just know fashion, I *am* fashion," said Tiffany, judging his outfit fail.

Mom could feel it was getting awkward and jumped in, "Tiffany, I love your clothes. I buy them for our daughters all the time."

"Then you have marvelous taste," Tiffany replied with a smile. "Girls, go get yourself some yummy smoothies and donuts while your parents and I get to work."

GEM Sisters munched at the snack table and waited for the other contestants to arrive.

"These donut sprinkles are giving me a

vision for a cute skirt design!" said Evangeline. She pulled out her sketchbook and started to draw.

"I've never heard anyone talk about sprinkles as fashion before," said a teen boy, laughing.

Behind them stood a cute 16-year-old with messy brown hair and brown eyes. His ripped jeans and wrinkled sweatshirt didn't match the squeaky clean lobby. He had a camera strapped around his neck.

"Hey! I'm Mason, Tiffany's son," he said, extending his hand to Giselle. "I'll be taking all the event pictures this weekend."

Giselle found herself tongue-tied. "I'm available! I mean available to you . . . for pictures, that is. I'm available for pictures."

Oh geez. Giselle was never very smooth when it came to talking to cute boys. She hoped she hadn't embarrassed herself too much.

"This is my good side," ordered Mercedes, pointing to her right cheek.

"You're GEM Sisters, aren't you?" asked Mason. "My mom showed me your videos. You girls are really funny."

"But seriously, did you hear me? This is my good side," repeated Mercedes.

"Got it," replied Mason. "How about you all give me your best model pose?"

Mason held up his camera and took their picture. As he left, he locked eyes with Giselle and flashed her a quick smile. Suddenly, she felt her interest in the contest being replaced by her interest in Mason.

Mercedes sipped on her second blueberry smoothie. She was excited to see the clothing racks by the snack table. Hung on the racks were black bags so you couldn't see the clothes inside. Each bag had a girls' name on it.

She wanted to sneak a peek at her outfit, but Mercedes couldn't risk getting caught. Instead, she crossed her fingers and hoped her outfit was better than everyone else's.

The sisters watched as contestants and their parents started to arrive. First was a beautiful, tall, redheaded girl with a very mean look on her face. Her father stood next to her and he looked even grumpier than she did.

"Stand straight, Fiona," snapped the angry dad. His daughter obeyed.

Next, a cute, curvy African American girl entered. She excitedly ran up to GEM Sisters. The smiling girl had fun pigtail braids with purple bows and a t-shirt that read "Make

Today Amazing."

"OMG! I didn't know GEM Sisters were going to be here. I watch your videos. Hi, I'm Jasmine," she said as she hugged Evangeline.

She quickly turned and hugged Mercedes, who was mid slurp on her third blueberry smoothie. Thankfully, the drink didn't spill on her dress because she hadn't brought a backup.

"Why hello there. I'm Jasmine's mom, Mrs. Harris. Are you girls in the contest?" she asked.

"Yes we are, but we're not entered as a group. So, it's each sister for herself," Giselle said with a laugh. No one got her joke or laughed back.

Jasmine was about to speak when her mom interrupted. "How about that? Ya know I'm a designer too, like Tiffany. This purse here is special and one of a kind. I whipped it up for the contest."

GEM Sisters looked at the mom's bright red purse that was covered in big, colorful beads. The beads formed a wild flower pattern on the large bag. It definitely was not the style of Totally Tiffany.

Mercedes and Giselle looked at each other and silently agreed. That purse put the "ugh" in ugly. Evangeline, on the other hand, liked how original it was.

Mrs. Harris handed the girls her business card. "If you want one of my purses for your videos, let me know," she said happily. "No two purses are alike."

"Thank goodness," whispered Mercedes to Giselle. "One is already too many."

The last few groups of girls excitedly entered the front door. The most dramatic entrance came from Ivy. She was better known as the social media icon "Ivy-Tastic" and had millions of followers.

Ivy had light blonde hair with big blue eyes and lots of makeup. She had on a midriff top showing off her belly button and wore small oval-shaped sunglasses. Ivy's snobby mother stood close by, filming her daughter.

"I'm here! Shout out to all my Ivy-Tastic fans in New York," said Ivy loudly as she blew kisses. "I brought a special treat for everyone. My world-famous puppy, Percy!"

What a showoff, Mercedes thought.

She watched as contestants ran up to take pictures with Ivy and her dog. Mercedes would never admit it, but Percy was the cutest Teacup Yorkie puppy she had ever seen.

Ivy noticed Mercedes and walked up to her.

"Eww! I heard a rumor that GEM Sisters were going to be here. Good thing Tiffany called an actual famous person. I'm going to win so you should leave," said Ivy.

"You wish! I'm a real model, so I'm going to win," interrupted the beautiful, red-haired girl named Fiona. Even without high heels, she was the tallest girl in the room.

"Excuse me?" said Ivy back to Fiona with a rude expression.

"You don't belong here. This is a contest for real models, not people who make kissy faces online," said Fiona with a sharp stare.

"Actually I do modeling on social media all the time! If you want to see influencers who are wannabe models, go watch GEM Sisters. Just sayin'," said Ivy with a mean scowl.

Mercedes' mouth dropped in shock. Things were getting ugly fast.

"I know who the GEM Sisters are, and they're NOT models," hissed Fiona.

"Hi, Fiona is it?" interrupted Mercedes with sass. "Sorry, never heard of you. Are you sure your big head is going to fit on that little stage?"

At that moment everyone saw that these three girls were in the lead for winning the contest. Fiona, Ivy, and Mercedes were equally bold and beautiful.

Ivy usually bullied her way to get whatever she wanted. But now she saw that Fiona and Mercedes were not scared of her. She was worried, but she tried not to show it.

"Everybody has the same chance of winning," said Jasmine, wanting to defend GEM Sisters. She didn't like it when people fought. Plus she wanted all the girls to feel good about the contest.

Ivy shot Jasmine an evil glare. "Hi, Miss Nobody. See those skinny girls on the posters up there? Do you look like any of them? No! You should go home because you have zero chance of winning."

"How dare you! Why you entitled little brat," said Jasmine's mom. Her face was red with anger.

Before she could continue, Tiffany took to the stage. "Hello sweeties! Thank you so much for coming. Who's ready to get beautiful?"

Everyone except Mercedes turned to watch Tiffany's speech. Instead, Mercedes looked up at the posters of the past years' models on the wall. Each year's winner seemed more beautiful than the last. They all had different shades of blonde or light brown hair, flawless skin, and perfect teeth.

No one looks like me either, thought Mercedes. *Uh oh!*

Jasmine tried to smile through it, but Ivy's words had definitely hurt her feelings.

Mercedes turned to her sisters. "Do you think I even have a chance of winning?"

"Shhh!" replied Giselle. "We're supposed to be listening."

"Huh?" answered Evangeline. "Hey Mercedes, you've got smoothie seeds in your teeth."

Mercedes' eyes darted around the room. Behind the racks of clothes she saw the bathrooms. She bolted past the snack table hoping to make it back by the end of Tiffany's speech.

"Totally Tiffany stands for . . . perfection," continued Tiffany. "The winner chosen this weekend must be the best in every area of the contest. She must look great in my clothes. She has to interview well on the red carpet, and have an amazing photo for her poster. And of course, she must have the best runway walk!"

The crowd cheered and clapped for Tiffany's speech. Meanwhile, Giselle and Evangeline were having second thoughts. They had hoped for a fun weekend with some cute clothes and new friends. This contest was a lot more serious than they had realized.

"One of you lucky girls will be chosen as the face of my new clothing line. The winner will be treated like a princess. You'll be flown around the world. Designs will be created just for you. You'll be on TV, in magazines, and on billboards from New York to Los Angeles to London and Dubai. The world will know your face."

Mercedes hurried back from the bathroom. She leaned over and whispered to her sisters. "I've decided I'm not giving up. I'm gonna do whatever it takes to win."

"That's the Mercedes I know and love," said Evangeline with a wink.

"I want someone to win who is NOT Ivy," added Giselle.

"There are twenty-two contestants here today. Each of you was chosen for a special reason," said Tiffany. "Some of you are models already like Fiona Murphy. Others are social media stars like Ivy-Tastic and GEM Sisters. And for some, this is your first time in the spotlight."

All of a sudden workers lined up next to the

clothing racks. The workers wore black clothes and looked very serious.

"Now sweeties it's time for the first part of the contest. The fitting!" squealed Tiffany. "Find the clothing bag with your name on it. There are only four dressing rooms so you'd better hurry!"

FWEET! FWEET!

The workers blew their whistles signaling it was "go time." Everyone was scrambling and bumping into each other. They all wanted to be the first to put on their outfits.

Giselle and Evangeline blinked and Mercedes was gone. Somehow, she already had her outfit bag in hand and was running to the dressing rooms. Close on her heels were Ivy, Fiona, and Jasmine with her mother.

Mercedes was out of breath as she ran into the first dressing room.

"Hurry, Jasmine! We have to beat those mean girls. There are only three dressing rooms left. Go!" yelled Mrs. Harris to her daughter.

She handed Jasmine the dress bag and gave her a nudge. Jasmine rushed over and almost made it to a dressing room when . . . Fiona burst past her and pushed her way inside.

"Oops, sorry. This is a contest, not a

friendship gathering," said Fiona. "I'm here to win!"

SLAM!

Jasmine brushed it off and headed to the fourth room. She wasn't going to let Ivy and Fiona bring her down. The girls scrambled to get dressed first.

Ivy shouted in a mocking voice, "You girls should stay in your dressing rooms. Cuz wow, look at me in this outfit! I'm the reason Tiffany became a designer."

Mercedes responded, "Ivy, how are you getting that little outfit over your giant mouth?"

Without warning, a scream filled the air.

"Oh no! My outfit is ruined!" cried Jasmine.

CHAPTER 2

"My beautiful dress is destroyed!" cried Jasmine.

Her scream brought all the girls from the contest over to the dressing rooms. Ivy, Fiona, and Mercedes popped out to see what was happening.

Jasmine's mom quickly rushed in to help her daughter. There were sounds of rustling clothes, Jasmine whimpering, and hushed talking. A moment later Mrs. Harris threw open the dressing room door.

Mrs. Harris held up Jasmine's stained dress, still half in its black bag. It was covered in some sort of dark blue goo that was now dripping on the floor. Jasmine's face was full of tears.

"Look what someone did to my poor daughter's dress!" yelled Mrs. Harris to the crowd.

Evangeline and Giselle watched in the line of girls waiting for the dressing rooms. They noticed several contestants checking their bags to make sure their outfits were okay.

Evangeline glanced at her sketchbook. Earlier she had used some blueberry smoothie to draw a cute skirt design. She had decorated the blue skirt with frosting from the donuts at the snack table.

"It looks like blueberry smoothie was poured on the dress," Evangeline whispered to Giselle.

"I think you're right," said Giselle, looking at her sisters' odd drawing. "And blueberry is an impossible stain to get out. That dress is toast!"

Mrs. Harris glared at Fiona, Ivy, and Mercedes. "One of you did this! You three girls think you're better than everybody else don'tcha? And you have Tiffany thinking the same thing."

She pointed to Mercedes.

"I've seen those prank videos you do to your sisters," argued Mrs. Harris. "Was this one of your funny pranks?"

"No," said Mercedes worriedly. "I didn't do this."

"You can't just blame us because you're

jealous," said Fiona with a smug face.

"I don't like you. And ya know what else? I don't trust you," continued Mrs. Harris. "You stole Jasmine's dressing room. Shameful!"

Ivy let out a giggle.

"Excuse me. This is funny to you? You've been nasty from the second you met my baby girl. Why do you think you're so much better than her?" demanded Mrs. Harris.

"Mom, can we just go?" asked Jasmine. "I don't want to blame anyone who didn't do it."

Jasmine figured one of the girls was lying, but she didn't like to argue. Her mother wasn't as forgiving.

Tiffany rushed onto the scene. Poor Mom and Dad were trying to keep up and not trip while filming.

"Oh my stars! What happened?" Tiffany asked, shocked.

Tiffany unzipped the clothing bag all the way and a fountain of dark blue smoothie splashed out. The once beautiful dress was soaked and could no longer be worn. Everyone wondered what she was going to do.

"Jasmine, sweetie, how did this happen?" asked Tiffany.

Choking back tears, Jasmine tried to speak

but was too upset. She did not like the pressure of the situation.

Mrs. Harris turned to Jasmine and said, "Come on now honey, it's okay. Tell Miss Tiffany what happened."

Jasmine squeezed her mom's hand and found her strength.

"I was excited to put on my outfit. My mom helped me grab my bag so I could hurry to the dressing room. When I arrived, Mercedes was already here with Ivy and Fiona," she explained.

Mercedes gulped. Somehow Jasmine's story was making it sound like the three of them were doing something bad together.

We got here early because we want to win, Mercedes thought. *What's wrong with that?*

Jasmine continued, "I was surprised that I got here fast enough to get to the last dressing room."

"Actually she was knocked out of her dressing room by that red-headed giant," said Mrs. Harris pointing to Fiona.

"Mama, I got this," said Jasmine. "When I started unzipping my bag, I saw my dress was all wet. It was covered in huge, dark blue stains. That's when I screamed."

"Are you sure you didn't drop the dress or maybe spill your smoothie on it when you were rushing?" said Tiffany in an unsure voice.

"Excuse me. My daughter has done nothing wrong," complained Mrs. Harris.

"Okay, settle down. I'm just not sure how to handle this," explained Tiffany.

"*These* are the girls you should be questioning!" replied Mrs. Harris angrily as she pointed to Ivy, Fiona, and Mercedes. "They've been hating on Jasmine all day."

Giselle and Evangeline knew Mercedes had not said anything mean to Jasmine. It wasn't fair to blame her. Still, they thought it best to stay quiet with everyone already being so upset.

"I'm sorry, but I've listened to enough of this woman," said Ivy's mother. "My daughter is a perfect angel."

"Oh really. If she's so perfect then why was she telling my daughter to go home?" asked Mrs. Harris in an upset tone.

Tiffany could tell things were bubbling out of control fast. "Everyone let's please try to talk calmly."

Fiona's dad could no longer be silent.

"My daughter is an award-winning model. Is this how she is going to be treated here?" he said.

GEM Sisters' mom stopped filming and put down her camera. "I agree. It's not fair to blame the girls if they didn't do anything wrong."

"Well sweeties," said Tiffany, turning to the three accused girls. "Did you do this?"

Ivy, Fiona, and Mercedes all shook their heads "no" together. It was the first and only time they all agreed on something. It was *that* serious.

"So now they get to lie and Jasmine doesn't have a dress. That's not fair," continued Mrs. Harris. "How's she gonna walk the runway?"

"Can all the parents please come with me?" ordered Tiffany as she led them out of the room.

Mrs. Harris told Jasmine to wait in her dressing room until she returned. She didn't want anything bad to happen to her while she was gone.

Dad followed Tiffany and kept filming. Mom stayed behind and huddled her three daughters together.

"Are you okay, Mercedes?" asked Mom.

"I guess. I don't know why Mrs. Harris is blaming me for ruining Jasmine's dress," answered Mercedes.

"Well she *is* right. You do like to pull

pranks," added Giselle.

"And you do lie all the time," said Evangeline.

"Whose side are you on?" questioned Mercedes.

Her sisters realized Mercedes wasn't in the mood to be teased.

"Mercedes, I need you to tell me the truth. Did you do it?" asked Mom.

"What? No!" Mercedes answered seriously. "I promise I didn't."

"Then I'm going to join the other parents and see what's happening. Giselle, keep your sisters out of trouble," Mom ordered as she ran off.

"I've tried," Giselle whispered to herself, "and it's not possible."

She wasn't the only one whispering. Around the room contestants started to chatter and spread rumors. Some of the girls thought Fiona had done it simply because she was mean. Others felt Ivy did it to stir up drama for attention.

Giselle overheard a girl with long brown hair standing near them.

"I think Mercedes did it because she's jealous," the girl whispered to her friend.

Nothing nice was being said about Ivy, Fiona, or Mercedes. The crowd seemed to agree with Mrs. Harris. One of them was responsible for ruining Jasmine's dress.

A few of the girls glared at Mercedes like it was her fault. It was an icky feeling and she didn't like it.

"I should not have drank so many smoothies. Now I look guilty," worried Mercedes.

"That's true," said Evangeline. "You did drink like a hundred of them."

Mercedes glared at her little sister.

"It's just a joke. Lighten up. OMGeezers!" groaned Evangeline.

"Well someone ruined Jasmine's dress and we need to find out who it was," urged Giselle.

"It's a case for the Sister Detectives!" exclaimed Evangeline.

"Hello? I'm trying to win this contest and become a famous model. I can't be a detective right now," complained Mercedes.

"Um, you're a suspect who is accused of being guilty of a crime," said Giselle in a serious voice. "You better make time."

Mercedes remembered other cases they had solved as the Sister Detectives. A suspect was the person who they thought might be responsible for doing something wrong. She didn't like it, but her sister was right. She *was* a suspect.

"Here's an idea," started Mercedes. "Let's make it look like Ivy is guilty. We can tell everybody she did it. She gets blamed and I don't have to deal with her anymore. Win, win!"

"That's called framing," said Giselle. "You can't frame Ivy!"

"I want to be framed," said Mercedes. "Why can't someone frame my picture?"

"No," explained Giselle. "*Framing* someone is when you make a good person look guilty. Framing by the way, is also a crime."

Whether it was right or wrong, Mercedes loved the idea of blaming Ivy.

"Fine. Let's solve the case. But we have to do it fast so I can focus on winning," commanded Mercedes.

Evangeline interrupted, "While you two were wasting time arguing, I went and got our first clue."

On Evangeline's finger was a blob of sticky goo. She took a lick.

"Is that from the smoothie puddle on the floor?" asked Giselle, making a yucky face.

"Of course! And I was right. It tastes exactly

the same as the blueberry smoothies we had at breakfast," explained Evangeline.

"So what? Everybody was drinking them this morning. Anyone could have poured the drink on Jasmine's dress," sighed Mercedes.

This meant everyone was a suspect. They still had zero clues.

"We need to think about *why* someone would want to destroy Jasmine's dress," explained Giselle.

Evangeline responded, "Ooh! I got it. Maybe someone here is an evil, undercover spy who works for a secret fashion club. The spy's mission was to sneak into the contest and destroy every Tiffany outfit one by one."

Mercedes usually found Evangeline's silly ideas entertaining, but not when she was in trouble.

"Do we think Jasmine might have ruined her own dress on purpose?" suggested Giselle.

"Well, I only ruin my outfits when mom buys me ugly clothes," said Mercedes. "But Jasmine's dress was super cute, so I don't think she would have done that."

"Then we're back to Ivy and Fiona as our main suspects for this mystery," said Giselle.

Mercedes raised her hand.

"I vote Ivy did it," she said a little too loudly.

"Why are you talking about me you little wannabe?" screeched Ivy.

Mercedes gasped, "I'm not a wannabe!"

"Everyone knows you want to be as famous as me," Ivy said with a smirk. "Good luck, cuz you never will be."

"Mind your own business!" hissed Mercedes.

"What-evs! I'm just repeating all the rumors I'm hearing," snapped Ivy.

Fiona joined the argument. "You're both wannabe models. Why don't one of you just admit that you did it? Then both of you can crawl back into your social media holes."

Mercedes, Ivy, and Fiona all started shouting at each other, causing Jasmine to come out of her dressing room.

"Stop fighting!" yelled Jasmine. "It's my dress that got destroyed and I'm very upset about it."

"Maybe somebody did you a favor," Ivy said rudely. "Now you can drop out of the contest."

Jasmine was about to say something back to Ivy when Tiffany and the parents entered the room.

"Attention!" said Tiffany with a sharp little clap. "I have an announcement to make."

31

Everyone gathered around Tiffany to listen. Mrs. Harris saw Jasmine was upset and quickly went to her side.

Tiffany continued, "In my ten years of running this contest, nothing like this has ever happened before. Until now, contestants have always respected and cared for my Totally Tiffany designs."

Some of the faces in the crowd grew worried. It sounded like Tiffany was going to cancel the contest.

"Of course, it's not fair what happened to Jasmine. Don't worry, an amazing new dress will be created before her photo shoot. My design team is already working on it."

"Good," replied Mrs. Harris with her arms crossed.

Then Tiffany turned to Fiona, Ivy, and Mercedes. "Someone definitely destroyed this dress. *If* that person confesses right now they won't be in as much trouble. This is your last chance to tell the truth."

The silence in the room felt very awkward as Tiffany waited for someone to come forward. No one did.

"Well, I didn't want to do this, but you leave me no choice," said Tiffany. "When I find out

who ruined the dress, they will be kicked out of
the contest."

CHAPTER 3

"Finally lunch!"

Evangeline may have said it, but everyone was thinking it. Lunchtime could not have come soon enough. All the contestants wanted to move past what had happened earlier, including GEM Sisters.

After the fitting, Tiffany made the girls change out of their designer outfits and back into their original clothes. She didn't want any more of her Totally Tiffany designs to be ruined.

The sisters stood in line waiting to grab a plate of food. Today was spaghetti with meatballs, which was one of their favorites.

"I'm still too upset to eat," complained Mercedes.

"Then more for me!" squealed Evangeline, piling her plate high with extra noodles.

Giselle scanned the room looking for someone.

"He's not here," said Mercedes.

"Who? I don't know what you're talking about," lied Giselle.

"Really, Giselle? We know about your crush on Mason," replied Mercedes with a smirk. "Don't deny it."

Giselle knew she was bad at lying so she stopped talking. She couldn't let her sisters find out that she had already looked at Mason's social media profile. There wasn't a single picture of a girlfriend!

The Sister Detectives found a quiet place to sit and discuss the case. Before they took one bite, they heard their mother's voice from behind them.

"I see you forgot to get a healthy salad, so I brought you some."

Mom set a giant bowl of green leaves on the table. The girls groaned as she scooped lettuce onto their plates.

"And Evangeline, why did you bring this? It was with our film equipment," said Mom as she pushed the heavy suitcase toward her.

"This is a fashion contest. Of course I brought my suitcase. It's my secret weapon!"

said Evangeline as if it was obvious.

Mom scooted in to sit by her daughters and kept her voice low.

"So listen. I'm just checking in. There are a lot of rumors spreading right now. Mercedes, you know what I'm talking about."

"I know Mom. And like I said, I didn't do it!" said Mercedes loudly.

"Shh! I know that, but people I'm filming are blaming you, Ivy, and Fiona," warned Mom. "Plus, the way Tiffany was bragging about you three in her opening speech this morning . . . well, it made the other contestants really jealous."

"That's not fair," said the Sister Detectives together.

"I know that. I'm not the bad guy," said Mom. "But one of those girls might be. So I have a strict rule for this weekend. Stay clear of those three troublemaking girls."

Mercedes looked at Mom, hurt. "Three?"

"Oh sorry, Mercedes. The *two* trouble making girls," realized Mom. "Promise me!"

"Yes mom," they all said at the same time.

"Is that your father in the food line with three hamburgers and NO salad? I don't think so, buster. Not on my watch," said Mom as she left.

With Mom gone, the girls continued discussing the case.

"Um, how are we supposed to do detective work if we can't talk to Ivy and Fiona?" asked Evangeline.

"I don't know!" snapped Mercedes. "Guys this is really serious. We need to find out who did this so I don't get kicked out of the contest."

"Calm down. We will figure this out. Let's start with what we know. We think Ivy or Fiona did it. The question is why," asked Giselle.

"To win. Duh!" stated Mercedes.

"They both already think they're the best, so how does it help them to win by pouring smoothie on Jasmine's dress?" asked Giselle.

"Maybe it wasn't them," said Evangeline in a serious voice. "This is New York. The whole city is full of rats. So, what if there's a group of rats that live here at Totally Tiffany HQ? They are trained fashion rats who work in the basement. And they have their own rat fashion line called Rat-Tastic!"

Evangeline leaned in and whispered. She didn't want the rats to hear.

"A while back this talented rat came up with a super cute dress design. But the drawing blew up into the air vents and onto Tiffany's desk. Tiffany stole the design and made the dress for Jasmine. The rats found out and vowed to get even. So today, they snuck into the lobby and poured smoothie on the dress. Case Closed!"

Evangeline popped a meatball into her mouth.

"Do you think the designer rat was a girl?" asked Mercedes.

"Probably," stated Evangeline.

"No! We are not building a case on fashion rats! Please be serious," ordered Giselle.

"Fine. Then it was a frame job!" said Evangeline in a bored voice. "Like Mercedes talked about doing earlier to Ivy."

"Do you think one of them made the other girl look guilty? Why? So they would get kicked out of the contest?" questioned Giselle. "Now that's a real possibility."

Giselle was lost in thought. She was trying to piece together what to do next.

"But which girl is framing who?" asked Giselle. "Did Fiona do it to get Ivy kicked out or is it the other way around?"

"It's totally Ivy!" whined Mercedes. "She acts all perfect when really she's a big ol' jerk-faced-meany-pants-sandwich with extra mustard!"

"I can't argue with that," agreed Evangeline. "And I don't like how she was mean to Jasmine."

"You can't accuse someone because you don't like them. You need proof," lectured Giselle. "We need clues based on facts. It's called evidence."

"Boring!" sighed Mercedes.

As she picked up her phone to surf social media, she bumped Evangeline's fork. Spaghetti sauce oozed onto the table into a bendy, curved puddle.

Giselle quickly grabbed a napkin to clean it up.

"No! It's art. Don't touch it! Can you see?" asked Evangeline.

They didn't.

"Look at the shapes. Down there by the drippy goo at the bottom? It's a simple dress design with a perfect octopus in the middle. I need to capture this."

Evangeline opened a page from her sketch book and pushed it down on the messy spaghetti sauce blob. When she carefully lifted the page it formed the exact sticky pattern in her book. She blew on the paper so it would dry faster.

"I still don't see an octopus. Maybe a jellybean," said Mercedes, trying to support her.

"Either way, what are you doing?" asked Giselle, hoping Mason was nowhere near to see her weird sister.

"You guys are here competing to be the next world famous model, but I have bigger plans," explained Evangeline.

Mercedes was confused. "What's bigger than becoming the face of Totally Tiffany?"

"I'll show you," said Evangeline as she put her suitcase on the table.

Inside, the suitcase was filled with colorful pom poms, several scraps of fabric, and a few of GEM Sisters' costumes and wigs from their videos.

"I'm going to become a fashion designer like Tiffany," proclaimed Evangeline. "My first clothing line is inspired by bright colors, fresh patterns, and food. After Tiffany sees my designs, I know she'll make me her designer-in-training."

Her sisters had learned that Evangeline lived by her own rules. She had clearly made up her mind already, which meant there was no stopping her now.

"But don't worry I'm still doing the runway contest and stuff with you guys," said Evangeline. "A good designer must know all the parts of the fashion business."

***

After lunch all of the models gathered inside the photo studio. The trendy room was decorated with neon colored murals on the walls. One hot pink wall had a painting of crazy oversized sunglasses.

Tiffany clapped to get everyone's attention.

"Sweeties, we got off to a bumpy start, but we are back on track. You have two more events today that I will be judging for the contest. And, of course, tomorrow you will get to rock the runway!"

The crowd cheered. Tiffany knew how to get them excited.

"This next part of the contest is all about how well you pose for the camera! But you won't just be taking pictures . . . no, no, no. Whoever wins the contest will have their special photo displayed in my lobby!" squealed Tiffany.

The posters that the girls had seen earlier were so huge. It was hard for them to imagine themselves blown up and being featured for all to see in the Totally Tiffany lobby.

"Now I want to introduce you to my son, Mason. He is very talented and will be your photographer today," explained Tiffany.

Mason stood next to his mom still wearing his wrinkled sweatshirt and ripped baggy jeans. Unlike Tiffany, he was the opposite of fashion.

Several girls in the crowd smiled at him with puppy dog eyes, including Giselle. Evangeline groaned. She didn't care about all that lovey-dovey stuff.

Mercedes cared more about keeping an eye on Fiona and Ivy. All three girls stood close to the front next to Tiffany so they could be her favorite.

Fiona glared. Ivy stuck out her tongue. Mercedes rolled her eyes at both of them. It was a mean stare down between the girls.

Tiffany continued, "Each of you models will get your hair and makeup done by my amazing glam squad. Then you'll put on your custom outfit and have your picture taken!"

Suddenly, Mrs. Harris broke through the back of the crowd. "But wait! My Jasmine doesn't have her dress."

Jasmine followed behind her mother shyly.

"Not to worry. Jasmine's new dress is getting extra special care. She'll have to take her pictures last, but I promise it will be worth the wait," encouraged Tiffany.

Mercedes leaned over and whispered to Jasmine. "Going last is a good thing. I'm the 'M' in GEM Sisters and I always say 'best for last.'"

Jasmine giggled. "I know. I've seen your videos. Thanks for saying that. I'm actually feeling—"

"Jasmine!" snapped her mom quietly with clenched teeth. "Don't be talking to her. She's the enemy!"

Mercedes backed away. She wished Mrs. Harris was nicer.

"Lastly, just a reminder, no posting pictures of my clothes on social media. Everyone must wait for the big reveal at the runway show tomorrow. Now sweeties, let's get beautiful!" shouted Tiffany.

Instantly the calm crowd turned into a crazy free-for-all. Girls ran to be the first in line to get glammed. Once again Mercedes, Fiona, and Ivy made it there before everybody else.

Fiona's dad stood by her, making sure his daughter's makeup and hair were being done to perfection.

"She needs more powder on her forehead," he spoke gruffly to the stylist.

At that moment, Mercedes wished she had someone to help her. She told her stylist that she didn't wear makeup so she had no idea what would look best.

"You don't wear makeup?" said Ivy in the chair next to her. "What a baby! Just sayin'."

"Jealous much? You *have* to wear makeup because without it you look like an ogre," said Mercedes with sass.

Mercedes decided to close her eyes and ignore Ivy. After all, she promised her mom that she wouldn't talk to her. The stylist went to work curling Mercedes' long hair.

Meanwhile, Evangeline watched the parents coach their daughters on different smiles for their pictures. One girl was practicing a serious face in the mirror.

"She looks like she's trying to hold in a fart," said Evangeline, giggling to herself.

"Quick, Evangeline! How's my breath?" said Giselle as she blew hot air in her face.

"Gross! You definitely need a mint," replied Evangeline, reaching into her suitcase.

She pulled out an old sticky mint covered in

fuzzy lint. Giselle made a grossed out face as she popped it into her mouth.

"Thanks!" she said excitedly as she sprinted off.

Having a crush is so weird, thought Evangeline as she opened her food designs sketchbook.

Mom and Dad followed Tiffany and filmed her as she judged the girls. As each contestant got ready, Tiffany carefully took notes on her clipboard.

On the other side of the room, Giselle was rushing to get to the photo studio. She chose not to get glammed, but instead to have more time taking pictures with Mason.

She did one final check in the mirror. Her Totally Tiffany outfit looked super cute. It was a dark jean skirt with a pastel yellow button up top. She turned and ran without looking.

CRASH!

Giselle slammed into Mason, knocking him to the ground.

"Whoa! Someone's excited about having their picture taken," joked Mason as he stood back up. "Don't worry, my camera's okay."

For a second Giselle thought about running away, but realized that would be even more awkward. Why was she so clumsy?

"I think you hold the record for getting ready the fastest," said Mason with a smile.

Giselle started to panic. Maybe she should have spent more time preparing. "Well, I uh—"

"No. I, um . . . I like you looking natural," he gently responded. "Fashion usually makes people look fake."

The two stood in silence for a moment, nervously smiling.

Mason spoke first. "Guess we better get your pictures taken before the model mob gets here. Give me your best silly face."

Giselle got in position. She shifted and posed over and over as Mason took pictures.

"How about a spin for the camera?" he asked.

Feeling bold, Giselle twirled in a circle. Then . . . she fell backwards, tripping over the light stand behind her. She lost her balance and tore down the photo backdrop as she fell.

BOOM!

It was a disaster. Tiffany and her parents rushed over to make sure that she was okay.

Giselle was embarrassed. She went to hide by her sisters. Meanwhile, Mom and Dad helped Mason set the lights back up.

"Wow. Have you figured out you're not a model yet?" asked Fiona to Giselle with a smirk. "Thanks for taking yourself out of the contest."

Mercedes was about to tell Fiona where she could put her dumb, rude face when she spotted Ivy. She was wearing the same hairstyle as Mercedes!

"You copied my hair!" she screamed at Ivy.

The two girls looked like twins both with curled hair and a small messy bun on top.

"Who's jealous now? It looks better on me anyway. Go change yours or else I'm gonna tell all of my followers that you copied me!" threatened Ivy.

Evangeline could tell a fight was about to happen. Quickly, she pulled her sisters back and led them into the bathroom to cool down.

As of right now, it was crystal clear to Mercedes and Giselle which girl was guilty of the dress crime. They both shouted her name at the same time.

"It's Fiona!"

"It's Ivy!"

CHAPTER 4

After the photo shoot ended, the models got ready for the next part of the contest . . . the red carpet!

Out front, the lobby buzzed with energy as workers set up for the event. They rolled out a long red carpet in front of a fancy photo background with the words "Totally Tiffany" written on it. Doorman Stan greeted news reporters as they arrived.

Back in the green room, models were getting dressed and glammed. Giselle joined her sisters in the dressing room to have a Sister Detectives' meeting.

"Mom and dad are busy filming in the lobby," said Giselle to her sisters. "I told them we're fine for the red carpet."

"Perfect! Now can you please tell us your plan to take down Ivy," Mercedes begged

Evangeline.

"It's simple. We get the guilty girl to confess she did it," exclaimed Evangeline.

"That's not a plan, that's impossible," whined Giselle. "I'm still waiting for Mercedes to confess that she stole my last piece of gum today."

"No I didn't," lied Mercedes.

"You're chewing it right now!" growled Giselle.

Evangeline explained that for her plan to work they needed to dress up in costumes and go undercover.

"I'm going to pretend to be a reporter and trick them into telling the truth," proclaimed Evangeline. She turned to Mercedes and asked her questions as fast as she could.

"Are you nervous for the red carpet?"

"No."

"Are you going to win this contest?"

"Of course."

"What's your favorite color?"

"Pink."

"Can I borrow a piece of gum?"

"Sorry, I took Giselle's last piece."

Mercedes gasped. She had been tricked into telling the truth.

"Ooh! You're like a sneaky truth wizard," said Mercedes in awe.

Evangeline opened her suitcase full of odd costumes, wigs, and jewelry.

"I'll be dressing up as the French fashion reporter Rosalee Rains. One of you will pretend to be my cameraman," commanded Evangeline.

"Not it!" said Giselle and Mercedes at the same time.

FWEET! FWEET!

A worker blew a loud whistle to get everyone's attention.

"Please gather for Tiffany's announcement," shouted the worker.

"We're out of time," realized Evangeline. "Giselle, you hold the camera. Mercedes, you convince Ivy and Fiona that I'm a famous reporter."

"But what about walking the red carpet?" asked Mercedes. "I still want to win!"

"You'll have time," promised Evangeline. "You might have to go last, but hey, best for last!"

The girls quickly joined the rest of the models.

All of the contestants were now wearing jeans with a Totally Tiffany pink t-shirt and matching heels. The girls looked exactly the same just with different hairstyles.

"Anyone else think it's strange we're all dressed alike?" whispered Giselle to her sisters. "It's kind of creepy."

Mercedes wasn't happy about dressing like everyone else, but at least her shirt was pink.

"I heard Tiffany does this to keep her new outfits a secret from the reporters," Mercedes whispered back.

Tiffany spoke after the room got quiet. "The last event today is not about clothes. For the red carpet, I will be judging on how well you answer questions and pose for pictures. Remember, the winner will be walking on red carpets all over the world."

For a moment Giselle wondered how Mercedes would have time to be a world famous model and be in GEM Sisters. It was definitely something she needed to ask her later.

Tiffany continued, "If you want tips, I suggest you look to Ivy-Tastic and GEM Sisters. They have a lot of experience and are great with interviews."

The sisters quickly felt everyone in the room staring at them with mad eyes. The parents didn't like Tiffany choosing favorites.

"Good luck sweeties!" shouted Tiffany as she blew kisses.

"Oh please," said Ivy to Mercedes. "Tiffany thinks you have it, but you don't. The red carpet is where I shine. I'm the expensive designer shoes, and you and your sisters are just cheap knockoffs!"

Mercedes replied with force, "You know what Ivy? It's a shame you can't Photoshop your personality. That might actually help you win."

Ivy rolled her eyes and walked away.

Just then Jasmine bounced into the room. She had finished her photo shoot in her newly designed dress. Her dark skin looked amazing against the bright teal color.

"Girl, you look fabulous times a million," said Giselle with a snap of her fingers.

"Thanks," said Jasmine. "Wow, those are some fancy shoes."

"Well, the cuter they are, the more they hurt," Giselle replied with a giggle.

Mrs. Harris entered and was immediately upset. Her face was almost as red as her ugly one-of-a-kind purse.

"Jasmine had to go last for her picture and now everybody else is already dressed?" she complained.

The worker explained that a moment ago Tiffany had given her announcement to the group. Mrs. Harris was angry that once again her daughter had missed out.

"You'd think Tiffany would have seen my daughter wasn't here," complained Mrs. Harris. "But I guess she doesn't notice anyone but her favorites. Being last isn't the best, it's the worst."

FWEET FWEET!

"Ladies, the red carpet will start in 15 minutes. Please be ready," announced the worker.

The announcement sent everyone into a panic with last minute touches.

Evangeline realized she had to hurry. She grabbed her suitcase and motioned for Giselle to follow her.

"Don't forget the plan," Evangeline called back to Mercedes. "I need to interview Fiona and Ivy so I can trick them into telling the truth."

***

FLASH! SNAP! FLASH!

Tiffany posed on the red carpet in a stunning white gown. All of the interviewers were talking fast and loud at the same time! The whole room was a ball of energy.

"I can't explain why I'm so good at fashion, sweeties. I just am. I have a gift for making girls beautiful," Tiffany said with a smile.

Mercedes stood off to the side with the models waiting for her turn. Her eyes darted around the room wondering where her sisters were.

"What's wrong fraidy cat?" asked Ivy in a mean voice. "Too scared to walk the carpet without your sisters?"

Before Mercedes could respond, Ivy pulled out her phone and started filming.

"Hey Ivy-nators! About to hit the red carpet. Just wanna remind you to always be positive and be yourself. Wish me luck."

Ivy blew a kiss into her phone and posted the video. She was so fake. Mercedes wished she could grab her phone and smash it into a million pieces.

"It's your fault we come late to zis event!" snapped a woman with a French accent in the crowd. "Cameraman Bob! Zis way! Move your booty!"

The high fashion woman pushed her way into the line of reporters. She wore a long black dress with big black sunglasses and had short blonde hair.

Following her was a tall man with black hair and a thick mustache. He wore a tan baseball hat and held a big video camera on his shoulder.

"How you wear such ugly clothes at zis Tiffany fashion show? What a disgrace. You go hide in zee background with zee camera. We must not scare zee pretty girls. Yes?"

The duo was causing everyone to stare. They were so loud that they were bothering both models and reporters. People wondered who these odd newcomers were. That's when Mercedes realized . . . they were her sisters!

"Make camera ready now you buffoon!" screamed the woman at her cameraman.

"Who in the world is that tragic pair?" asked Fiona with a mean look.

"That's Rosalee Rains. She's like the biggest fashion reporter in France," lied Mercedes. "I overheard Tiffany talking to my parents about her."

"Oh wait, of course I know Rosalee Rains," lied Fiona. "She interviewed me at a fashion show in London last year."

Mercedes knew Fiona was lying, but she said nothing. Evangeline's plan was working.

"Then she's definitely going to wanna interview me. I have more followers than anyone else here," bragged Ivy.

Giselle, dressed as Bob, leaned in and whispered to Evangeline. "You better back it down or we're gonna get caught."

Rosalee took out her microphone and hit Bob on the head. "I do reporter job not you! Now, hold zee camera you fool!"

"Tiffany darling! It's me Rosalee Rains! Darling, so good to see you. You look zee mostest fabulous in zis dress! I have zee questions for you."

While Rosalee was interviewing Tiffany, the workers prepared Ivy, Fiona and Mercedes to go next onto the carpet.

"No way! Jasmine had to go last for the photos. You should let her go first," demanded Mrs. Harris.

The worker felt bad for Jasmine and lifted the red rope so she could go next.

But before she could go, both Ivy and Fiona bolted onto the carpet. Neither wanted Jasmine to go first. Mercedes felt bad, but she also wanted to win. She ducked under the rope and ran out to join them.

Jasmine wasn't surprised Ivy and Fiona cut in front of her. However, she was hurt that Mercedes did it too.

"You gonna let those little cheats get away with that? You said Jasmine could go first!" shouted Mrs. Harris.

"I'm sorry, they're already on the carpet. I can't pull them off. Jasmine can go next I promise," said the worker.

"It's fine, mama," said Jasmine. "Now I can study their poses and make sure I do something different."

Mrs. Harris hugged her daughter. "You go out there and shine. You got this."

Back on the carpet Ivy, Fiona, and Mercedes were in a pose-off! Each girl looked amazing and they knew it. Tiffany watched and smiled proudly.

Next up for interviews, the girls each talked to different reporters. They answered question after question about their favorite jewelry, hair products, and why they loved the Totally Tiffany clothing line.

"Ivy-Tastic! Darling! Over here! Come here my darling!" shouted Rosalee Rains.

"Hi, I'm Ivy and I have over a million followers," she said with a smile.

"What smell iz you? Zis odor you wear I can not place. But zis iz a good stink."

Ivy was confused by her question and replied, "Oh you mean like perfume? It's my cotton candy lotion, my favorite scent. I wear it every day."

"In France we like every zing to be blueberry."

"Blueberry isn't really my favorite. Just sayin'," replied Ivy.

Rosalee was about to ask Ivy another question when Fiona interrupted.

"Hi, I'm a huge fan of yours Rosalee. My name is Fiona Murphy."

This was not part of Evangeline's interview plan. For her questions to get to the truth, she needed one girl at a time. Now, both girls were talking at once.

"So zis contest are you zee winner you think?"

"Of course!" they both said at the same time.

"Actually, I'm going to win," interrupted Mercedes with sass.

Bob peeked out from behind his camera to glare at Mercedes. What was she doing?

Mercedes' job was to get them to the interview, not be in it!

"Um . . . sorry darlings. There iz so many of you for zee questions. I uh—"

Bob tapped Rosalee on the shoulder. When she didn't respond he tapped harder.

"You dufus! Bob! You are ruining zis interview!" complained Rosalee.

Bob whispered into Rosalee's ear. "Mom is onto us. She's headed this way. We gotta go now!"

Evangeline wasn't going to leave without getting answers. She had to think fast. She held out her microphone to Ivy, Fiona, and Mercedes.

"Who is zis Jasmine zat Tiffany talked so much about with me? I think she iz the winner zis year."

"What? Her? No way," scoffed Ivy.

"Only a real model like me is gonna win this contest," threatened Fiona. "If I have to, I'll make sure she doesn't win."

Bob cleared his throat. He motioned to Rosalee that Mom was only a few steps away.

"Great darlings. Toodles!" said Rosalee hurriedly. "Iz no more time. Iz how you say . . . poof!"

Rosalee and Bob ran off in a hurry. They may have cut the interview short, but Fiona's answer was all the proof they needed.

Fiona was guilty!

CHAPTER 5

"Welcome back ladies," said Doorman Stan as he opened the door for GEM Sisters.

Today was the big runway show. Most of the models had been practicing since they woke up. They were beyond ready to get started.

The sisters entered the grand ballroom where everyone was waiting. They saw a giant stage with stunning red theater curtains. A long runway surrounded by chairs stretched out from the stage.

"That runway is so long you could land an airplane on it," joked Evangeline.

Giselle felt instantly nervous. Being klutzy meant she would most likely trip and fall. She thought about quitting, but there was no backing out now.

The three sisters sat together and watched the workers prepare for the big event.

Spotlights were being turned off and on. The DJ tested the volume with upbeat dance music.

The Sister Detectives scanned the room, but there was no sign of Fiona.

"Let's just tell Tiffany what Fiona said," whispered Mercedes. "That's enough to get her kicked out of the contest!"

"It only shows she's mean and nasty," said Giselle. "It's not proof that she's guilty. We need to catch her doing something wrong or have clues to show that she did it."

Some parents were making their daughters practice walking while others chatted. Mrs. Harris sat with a group of parents holding a new ugly purse.

Her purse was light gray with rainbow straps. On the front, she had sewn on yellow beads in a zigzag pattern and a giant purple daisy flower. Evangeline loved wild style, but even she thought it was a bit much.

"Here's my card. My purses are all original designs. If you want to buy one, they make great gifts," said Mrs. Harris with a smile.

The parents kindly took the cards, but their faces were saying "not interested."

Mercedes made eye contact with Jasmine, who frowned and looked away. Evangeline noticed Jasmine was upset.

"I'm gonna go ask her what's wrong," said Evangeline.

"No, wait!" begged Mercedes.

She thought about lying to her sisters, but decided she should tell them the truth. After all, what she had done wasn't really that bad . . . was it?

"Um, yesterday on the red carpet Jasmine was supposed to go first, but we all cut in front of her. I only did it because Ivy and Fiona did," justified Mercedes.

Her sisters were surprised by Mercedes' actions. They knew she could be sassy and tell little lies to them, but she had never hurt a GEM before.

"We're the Sister Detectives. The whole reason we're working this case is to help Jasmine," said Giselle, confused.

"I know, but I want to win the contest too. Ivy and Fiona are doing whatever it takes to win. And sometimes that means not being nice," snapped Mercedes.

"Not cool, Mercedes," said Evangeline, as she went over to sit by Jasmine.

"If you act like bad people then that makes you one of them," warned Giselle as she got up and moved seats.

Ivy noticed Mercedes sitting alone. She grabbed her puppy Percy and shuffled over to her.

"Ooh sister drama! Looks like your own sisters can't stand you," taunted Ivy. "Just sayin'!"

Mercedes thought about what Giselle had told her. She tried to not say anything, but Ivy was asking for it.

"At least I have sisters. All you have is your dog who, by the way, is cuter than you," said Mercedes with attitude.

FWEET! FWEET!

A worker blew the whistle to get the crowd's attention.

Tiffany strutted onto the stage. Mom and Dad filmed every move as she turned, twirled, and flipped her hair. At the end of the runway, she flashed a smile and grabbed the microphone.

"That, my sweeties, is how you make an entrance!" squealed Tiffany.

The models clapped with delight. This was the part of the contest they had all been waiting for.

"Your runway walk counts for half of

your score. And why? Because it's the most important. This is where you make my clothes come to life!"

Just then Fiona stepped out onto the stage.

"I have asked Fiona to show you what I'm expecting to see in all of your runway walks," explained Tiffany.

Dance music started to play. Fiona stepped forward and began her model walk down the runway. She was a pro, taking strong, bold steps as she kept a serious face.

The parents were whispering angry things to one another.

"Looks like Tiffany has already chosen the winner."

"My daughter can do better than that."

Fiona reached the end of the runway. She posed three times then walked back.

Tiffany clapped. "Perfect! Girls, do exactly that."

"She's amazing," Giselle whispered to Evangeline. "No wonder she thinks she can get away with anything."

All of the contestants felt nervous after seeing Fiona on the runway. She was right. She was a real model. And right now Fiona had the best chance of winning.

Evangeline was the only girl not worried. She had already planned to fall back on her designing career. For her, today was only about having fun.

"Remember, the greatest thing about being a girl is her clothing. So, when you're on that runway, let your outer beauty shine!" commanded Tiffany.

Jasmine felt troubled by what Tiffany had told them. She leaned over and whispered to Evangeline.

"Do some of the things that Tiffany says bother you?"

Evangeline thought about it. "Yeah kinda. I love fashion, but they're just my clothes, not me."

"I think girls are strong and beautiful in their own way, but I feel like Tiffany wants us all to be the same," said Jasmine, concerned.

Giselle overheard the two talking. She wrapped her arms around them and gave them a big hug.

"I think both of you are pretty special just the way you are," she said with a smile.

Tiffany continued her announcement into the microphone.

"Sweeties! I need all models backstage. My

workers are waiting to give you the new heels you'll be wearing tonight with your Totally Tiffany outfit. It's practice time!"

"Heels again?" whined Jasmine. "Girls with big feet and heels don't mix!"

"Neither do heels and clumsy girls like me," giggled Giselle.

The models went backstage to get fitted for their shoes while their parents waited out front. Soon after, the runway practice began.

Fiona stood first in line followed by Ivy and Mercedes.

"Tiffany wants you to watch how I do this. Because, well . . . I'm the best," Fiona said rudely.

"You can walk without falling down? OMG! Who cares," Ivy said with a mean tone. "You'll both see who the real star is when it's my turn."

"Less talking and more walking ladies," ordered Mercedes.

Fiona took off first. Once again she owned the runway. She strutted boldly to the end, posed three times, and then walked back.

Ivy decided to add some cute factor to her walk by bringing along her puppy. She posed with Percy in her arms. Tiffany loved it so much that she told her workers to add Percy to the show.

It was Mercedes' turn to show her stuff. Her face was serious and her runway walk was fierce. As she shook her sassy hips, all eyes were on her. Tiffany tried to hide it, but her eyes popped. Mercedes was fabulous!

Mercedes couldn't help but smile. She was so proud of how the crowd was reacting.

Backstage, Giselle, Evangeline, and Jasmine practiced walking in their high heels. Instead of models, they looked more like little old ladies shuffling across the street.

"At this pace it will take us two years to get down the runway," joked Evangeline.

"Why do I feel like I'm going to trip even when I'm standing still?" worried Giselle.

"Maybe we should give up now," said Jasmine, sitting down and kicking off her pointy shoes.

"No! We can't let the evil shoes win. That's what they want!" said Evangeline in a serious tone.

Evangeline took off her heels and pretended they were fighting one another.

"We will take over the world one foot at a time! Moo Ha Ha!" said Evangeline in an evil voice.

"You guys crack me up so much!" said Jasmine, laughing.

"Jasmine!" yelled Mrs. Harris, as she ran up to their group. She put her arm around her daughter and pulled her away from her friends.

"Baby, you gotta stay focused. Those GEM girls don't really care about winning cuz they're already famous. But you're here to win!" said Mrs. Harris.

"Yes, Mama. Sorry," murmured Jasmine.

"Now get your shoes back on and get back to practicing," ordered Mrs. Harris.

Giselle and Evangeline realized a few other parents had also snuck backstage to coach their daughters.

"Back straight!" said one dad.

"Slower, don't rush it," said another mom sternly.

"You got this. You'll be Tiffany's favorite with that strut."

Until that moment they hadn't thought about how important this contest was to the other girls. They also understood why Mercedes wanted to win so badly. Regardless, what Mercedes had done to Jasmine at the red carpet was still wrong.

They watched as Jasmine's mom gave her

a hug and left. Giselle liked how Mrs. Harris supported her daughter even though she was hard on her.

"Evangeline! Giselle!" yelled a worker. "You're next!"

Fiona, Ivy, and Mercedes came backstage after their turns. Each of them felt like their runway walk was Tiffany's favorite.

"Excuse me, real stars coming through," Ivy said with a grin, carrying her puppy in her arms.

"How sad you have to use your puppy to get points. Your dog better not poop on the runway," jabbed Fiona.

As Giselle and Evangeline were walking to the stage, Mercedes made eye contact with them. She wanted to tell her sisters what a great job she had done. Instead, she looked away. They were probably still upset with her.

Mercedes turned and joined the mean girl talk. "I wonder if you can die from jealousy. I guess we'll see when I'm chosen as the winner."

Jasmine couldn't listen any longer. She had to say something.

"Stop it! As girls we should build each other up. Why do you three always have to tear into each other? We should all be friends."

"Real models don't need friends. And real models . . . wear heels," said Fiona, looking down at Jasmine's bare feet.

"Ew! I would definitely cover my feet if they looked like yours," said Ivy in a rude voice.

Mercedes saw Jasmine's face get upset. She wanted to stand up for her, but Jasmine walked away before she could.

Meanwhile, Giselle and Evangeline had no idea what was happening with Jasmine backstage because they were rocking the runway.

First Evangeline popped out onto the stage with a big happy smile. Her walk looked more like a fun dance. She did chugga chugga dance moves all the way down the runway and back.

Mom and Dad giggled as they filmed their silly daughter having fun.

Next was Giselle. She took a deep breath and started her strut. *Don't fall, don't fall, don't fall,* she thought over and over again.

Giselle noticed Mason was taking a lot of extra pictures of her.

At the front of the runway, Mrs. Harris looked angry sitting next to the other parents. Close by, Tiffany marked things on her clipboard as Giselle did her three poses and headed back.

All of a sudden a worker came out and stopped the music. "Jasmine's teal shoes are missing! We've looked everywhere and we can't find them."

Jasmine came out on stage looking upset. Mrs. Harris instantly shot up from her seat, angry. Tiffany knew she had better deal with this issue fast.

"Not to worry sweeties!" said Tiffany. "We have plenty of extra heels. Let's continue practice while my workers help her find a different pair."

"You know those girls probably stole them," said Mrs. Harris to Tiffany.

"Shoes get lost. It's nothing to worry about," said Tiffany calmly. She did not want Mrs. Harris to lose her temper again.

Tiffany started up the music. "Let's run it from the top!" she shouted.

Fiona, Ivy, and Mercedes were lined up waiting to go. Ivy decided that this time she would steal the spotlight. She pushed her way in front of Fiona and went first.

Mercedes knew how angry Fiona was, but she also knew that in order to win she had to go next. Before Ivy returned, Mercedes shoved her way past Fiona and jetted onto the runway.

Ivy bumped into Fiona on purpose as she walked backstage. Fiona scowled as Ivy pulled out her phone to film.

"Hey Ivy-nators! I like, totally rocked the runway. Can't wait for you to see me in full glam tonight!"

Fiona looked daggers at Ivy. She was sick of her games. However, she wasn't going to let Ivy get in her head. Mercedes returned and Fiona boldly stepped onto the runway as she had many times before.

"I did such a better job than that Fiona girl," said Ivy as she turned the camera to show the runway behind her. "She thinks she's the best, but we all know it's me!"

Fiona was almost to the front of the runway when all of sudden she slipped and fell.

THUD!

She landed hard on the runway.

"Ow!" cried Fiona. "Oh no! My ankle is broken!"

CHAPTER 6

Runway practice had ended early due to Fiona's fall. A doctor came to look at her ankle. He told her that luckily it was just sprained and not broken. That meant Fiona could still walk in the runway show that evening.

Meanwhile, the contestants gathered in the lobby with their parents. In front of the building was a big black shuttle bus. Everyone thought they were going to a fancy restaurant for lunch.

"I hope we're going out for pizza because I'm starving," whined Evangeline. "Walking on the runway takes a lot more energy than you think."

While they waited, the room was buzzing with rumors. Everyone was talking about Fiona's fall.

"I heard Mercedes tripped Fiona on

purpose," whispered one girl.

"Well Fiona deserves it. That girl thinks she's so much better than all of us," complained a different girl.

The parents were also spreading gossip in hushed voices.

"I never liked that girl anyway," grumbled one mom.

"Hey, at least our daughters will have a chance to win now," another mom hinted.

Giselle wasn't a big fan of Fiona, but she did not like people talking behind her back.

Mercedes sat alone pretending to scroll on her phone. Her sisters could tell she was upset that people were saying she had hurt Fiona on purpose.

"Should we go talk to her?" asked Giselle.

"Give her a minute," said Evangeline. "I can tell she wants to be left alone."

Since they shared a bedroom at home, Evangeline knew practically everything about Mercedes. This was her *don't-talk-to-me* face.

"Then let's split up and do some detective work," ordered Giselle. "You go spy over by Fiona and I'll snoop around the room."

To get closer to Fiona, Evangeline acted like she was drawing in her sketchbook. She leaned her head in to listen.

Fiona's ankle was wrapped in a tan bandage. Her dad put on a new ice pack to help with the swelling. She winced in pain.

"Sorry. I didn't mean to press so hard," said Fiona's dad.

"It's okay. It feels more cold than painful," replied Fiona.

Her dad got a serious look on his face. "Maybe you should quit. You don't have to compete."

"No! I want to stay," begged Fiona. "I don't know what happened. When I slipped it felt like there was ice or oil or something slippery on the runway."

"Maybe you stepped in something backstage and it got on the bottom of your shoe?" suggested her father.

"I don't think so. I'm just so thrown off because of those mean girls," said Fiona as she started to cry.

Evangeline wondered if Fiona was right. Maybe there was something on the runway that made her slip. And maybe it was still there!

FWEET! FWEET!

"Can I have everyone's attention?" shouted a worker.

Tiffany entered the lobby. She stood in front of the group looking more concerned than usual.

"This weekend has been full of surprises," Tiffany said with a tired sigh. "But for lunchtime today I have a special treat. We're having lunch at the spa!"

The room broke out in cheers. Everyone's mood instantly changed.

Tiffany continued, "Grab the spa bag with your name sewn on it and head to the bus. Parents you're staying here. But for you, we have a huge taco bar with every topping you could dream of."

Mom and Dad were told to stay behind and film the taco party. The spa was just for the girls. As for Dad, he'd choose tacos over spas any day.

Parents hugged their daughters goodbye as they filed onto the bus.

Evangeline ran up to Giselle. "I've got a feeling about something. I'm gonna go check it out. Stall them!"

Before Giselle could answer, Evangeline ran off.

"Where's she going?" asked Mercedes.

Giselle just shrugged her shoulders. They

both grabbed their spa bags and got onboard.

Slowly, the models filed in and found a seat.

Mercedes took a whole bench just for herself. She stretched out her legs and watched videos on her phone.

Giselle stared out the window and groaned, "Where are you Evangeline? The bus is about to leave."

She was always having to look out for her little sister.

In the back of the bus Ivy was surrounded by girls. They were all huddled over her phone watching a video and giggling.

"I love this part," laughed Ivy as she played back Fiona falling down on the runway. "Look! She has no idea she's about to crash and burn."

Fiona was sitting in the front, but the group was so loud she could hear every word.

Jasmine couldn't help but feel bad for her. Fiona may have been rude, but no one deserved to be made fun of for getting hurt.

"Mind if I sit by you?" asked Jasmine.

"Why, so you can make fun of me too?" snapped Fiona.

"Of course not. When I'm upset I get happier being around my friends," said Jasmine. "Real models need friends too."

"Why would you want to be my friend? I was so mean to you," said Fiona.

"Because I think you're amazing and super talented," replied Jasmine. "Wanna listen to the new single from Hometown Boyz with me?"

"That's my favorite band," said Fiona with a smile.

"Me too!" squealed Jasmine as they sat together.

Jasmine handed Fiona one of her earbuds.

"I've never met someone like you," Fiona said in a serious tone. "I'm in a lot of contests and I've learned you have to act mean to win. I'm really sorry."

"Well I can only forgive you because you like Hometown Boyz," Jasmine said with a giggle.

The new friends hummed along to the music.

"Okay sweeties!" shouted Tiffany as she stepped onto the bus. "Time to go to the spa!"

"Wait for me!" hollered Evangeline as she hopped on. She plopped down next to Giselle, holding her sketchbook tight. "I got the proof!"

"What proof?" asked Giselle.

"Tell you later," Evangeline said with a wink.

***

A soothing vanilla scent greeted the girls as they walked into the spa. Light flooded in from the skylights in the ceiling. Fancy statues and beautiful potted plants decorated the white walls. There was a bubbling fountain in the front lobby and soft harp music filled the air.

"This place is paradise," gushed Mercedes. "I'm never leaving."

In the locker room, the girls opened their personal spa bags. Inside they found comfy white robes, slippers, and face masks. Every item had their name on it just like their special bag.

"We are totally making a haul video with these when we get home," said Giselle as she put on her robe and slippers.

The girls were all smiles as they found their way to the different spa stations. They could choose from facials, manicures, foot rubs, and hair oil wraps.

For Evangeline, none of those things compared to the room filled with snacks and a giant chocolate fountain. There were piles of marshmallows, graham crackers, strawberries, and pieces of pineapple on sticks.

"Is this real? Quick! Someone pinch me," begged Evangeline.

Giselle reached over and gave her arm a squeeze.

"Ow! It is real," said Evangeline excitedly as she filled up her plate.

All of a sudden Evangeline smelled a familiar odor.

Oh great. Thought Evangeline. Ivy's ruining the food with her cotton candy lotion scent.

She looked around the room, but Ivy was nowhere. Evangeline leaned over to sniff Mercedes.

"It's you!" whined Evangeline. "Why do you smell like Ivy?"

Mercedes sniffed herself. "What? I don't know. It must have rubbed off on me. Ivy puts on buckets of that cotton candy stuff. I bet it's on all of us."

Evangeline smelled her hands and hair. "Well I don't stink like her."

"Gosh! Why are you being so rude?" shouted Mercedes. "Fine! I'll go wash my hands."

Mercedes stormed out of the room in a huff.

"What was that about?" asked Giselle.

"We need to talk," urged Evangeline. "I think Mercedes did something bad . . . like really bad. I'm worried that she—"

"Sweeties! You can't just hang around the snack table," pleaded Tiffany. "Go get your nails painted! I love your fabulous nails in your GEM Sisters' videos."

The two Sister Detectives knew they would have to talk later. For now they did as Tiffany asked and went to the nail station.

The walls inside the room were filled with every color of nail polish you could imagine. The sisters picked their favorite colors then went to sit in comfy chairs next to Jasmine and Fiona.

"If you press this button on the remote, the chair rubs your back," explained Jasmine. "It feels so good!"

They each pressed the button on their chairs.

The girls said together in a relaxed voice, "Awww."

Mercedes entered the room. She picked a light pink glitter polish and sat in the last open chair. Her sisters could tell from the look on her face that she was still mad.

"Neon orange? Wow Jasmine, that's a really bold choice," Ivy said with a smirk as she strolled in. "Better not lose your shoes again cuz Tiffany will want to cover up that color. Just sayin'."

Ivy flipped her hair and strutted out of the room.

"I wish there was an app I could download to mute her," said Mercedes with sass.

"Don't listen to her Jasmine," declared Giselle. "Your toes are poppin' with that cute color."

"I'm so jealous of how good that neon orange looks against your skin," encouraged Fiona. "I wish I could wear it."

Then Fiona's voice turned serious.

"Actually, if I'm being honest, I wish I was naturally pretty like you guys," said Fiona with a sad sigh. "I have to wear makeup to cover up my freckles."

"Freckles?" the girls replied at the same time.

"You can't see them because I put on tons of makeup," said Fiona, getting emotional. "As a model I get made fun of by other girls. They call me 'speckle face'. It's embarrassing."

Small tears started to stream down Fiona's face. Jasmine handed her a tissue. As Fiona wiped her cheek, it revealed a cluster of freckles under her makeup.

Fiona continued, "When I was younger I loved my freckles. I felt like they were a special part of me. But I've learned that being a model means I have to hide what makes me different. So, every day I cover them up."

"I'm sorry to hear that. If it makes you feel better I wish I wasn't so tall," said Giselle. "I'm always taller than the boys I like. And I'm so skinny. I want curves like Evangeline."

"No way Giselle. These curves are all mine," joked Evangeline. "But you can have my big poofy hair. It's like trying to tame a wild animal on top of my head every day."

"And what's with picking on girls who have thick eyebrows?" asked Mercedes, joining in. "I mean, hello! Every person in the world has eyebrows. We're born this way!"

The girls in the room clapped for Mercedes. They didn't notice, but Tiffany was standing nearby. She was pretending to be busy on her phone. Actually, she was listening as the girls talked honestly to one another.

Several other girls in the room heard what they were talking about and joined in.

"I wish my nose was smaller."

"My lips are so thin. I hate it."

"I would give anything to be skinnier."

"People say I have big ears."

"I don't want to wear glasses, but I have to."

"Why does my forehead have to be so big?"

Jasmine stood up and addressed the group. "You know what, we need to stop putting ourselves down. Each of us is beautiful and special in our own way."

"I totally agree," said Giselle. "All of us are GEMS! We're perfect just the way we are."

Jasmine grabbed a fresh makeup wipe from the counter and handed it to Fiona.

"What do you say?" she said looking into her friend's eyes. "Can we meet the real you?"

Fiona thought for a second. Slowly she started wiping her cheek. Quickly her natural face was revealed, freckles and all.

The girls oohed and aahed at her rare beauty. Fiona's freckles and bright red hair made her stand out even more. Her true self was shining bright.

"Next stop, facials!" cheered Fiona.

The group of girls rushed out of the room happily chatting.

"Are you coming?" Giselle asked Mercedes.

"No, I need a deep oil hair remedy. I'm not allowing these split ends on the runway," groaned Mercedes as she walked away.

"Giselle, follow me," whispered Evangeline. "There's something I need to show you."

Since all of the girls were busy getting spa treatments, the quiet locker room was the perfect place to talk.

"What I'm about to tell you is shocking," started Evangeline. "You know how Mercedes has been acting strange. Well, I think it's because she's behind all of the bad stuff going on."

"That's crazy," blurted Giselle. "No way."

Evangeline stated the facts. Mercedes drank several blueberry smoothies. She left the lobby right before Jasmine's dress was ruined. She was backstage when Jasmine's shoes were stolen. Finally, Mercedes smelled like cotton candy lotion today.

"Why does Ivy's lotion make Mercedes guilty?" asked Giselle.

"Sniff this," said Evangeline as she opened up her sketchbook to a sticky page.

"It smells like cotton candy," said Giselle. "So what?"

"I think Mercedes stole the lotion from Ivy. She used it to make Fiona trip on the runway," said Evangeline.

She explained how Fiona had told her dad

that it felt like she had slipped on some type of liquid. So, before getting on the bus, Evangeline had snuck back to the runway to check for clues.

On the runway, Evangeline found a gooey blob of lotion. She used a sheet of paper in her sketchbook to soak up the goo.

The Sister Detectives had to face the facts. Mercedes was now a suspect.

Meanwhile, Mercedes was getting ready to leave the hair station when Ivy stormed in. She shoved her way past Mercedes and sat in the chair.

Ivy spoke in a mean voice to the worker, "I talked to your boss and she said you would mix up a special coconut hair oil just for me."

"I don't think we have that oil," replied the worker as she scanned the row of bottles.

"Then go talk to your boss and figure it out," said Ivy in a snotty voice.

The worker quickly left the room.

"Someone should teach you a lesson in manners," warned Mercedes.

"Why? It's her job. Now stop talking to me loser. I need to relax," commanded Ivy. "Byeeee!"

Ivy laid her head back in the shampoo bowl.

She took two cucumbers and placed them on her eyes. Then she popped in her earbuds and listened to her favorite music.

Mercedes wasn't surprised by Ivy's rudeness. There were literally a hundred bottles of hair products on the counter she could have used.

Mean thoughts about Ivy ran through Mercedes' head. She glared at her dumb face and perfect blonde hair.

"I hope your hair turns out horrible," Mercedes whispered in a mean tone.

***

A while later, back at the locker room, most of the contestants had changed out of their robes and back into their clothes.

Mercedes tucked her slippers into her bag. She was about to ask her sisters if they were ready to get on the bus when—

"Aaaaaahhh!!!" screamed Ivy as she ran into the locker room.

"Aaaaaahhh!!!" screamed everyone else when they saw her.

They all stared in shock. Ivy's blonde hair had been dyed green!

"You did this!" screamed Ivy at Mercedes.

Ivy shook with anger. She was so mad she shoved Mercedes.

"Don't touch me!" yelled Mercedes.

"I can do whatever I want, you sneaky little liar!" shouted Ivy.

Mercedes paused for a second. Without thinking, she charged like an angry elephant. She shoved Ivy so hard she fell into the wall of lockers behind her.

"Fight!" yelled the girls, many of whom already had their phones out filming.

The enemies shoved each other back and forth. The girls cheered on as they fought.

Mercedes reached for Ivy's green hair and started pulling. Ivy lost her balance and fell on one knee. As Ivy lunged to get up, she made a mad grab for Mercedes. She pulled on Mercedes' bag and yanked it hard. The bag burst open.

GASP!

Out of Mercedes' bag spilled:
- Green hair dye.
- Cotton candy lotion.
- Jasmine's teal shoes.

Evangeline was right. Mercedes was guilty.

CHAPTER 7

Mercedes sat alone at the front of the bus. Each girl entered, looked at her angrily, and walked past. Ivy, with her green hair, glared without saying a word. Mercedes found her silence even more upsetting.

Tiffany stood outside of the bus talking to Giselle and Evangeline. Mercedes tried to make out what they were saying, but she couldn't read lips. She didn't need to. Tiffany's face said it all. She was furious.

A big black limousine pulled up. Tiffany hopped inside, then rode away.

Giselle and Evangeline were the last ones on the bus. They sat down slowly in the seat next to Mercedes.

"What were you guys talking about?" asked Mercedes. "What's gonna happen?"

"It's not good, sis," said Evangeline softly.

"Tiffany is heading back first so she can talk to the parents."

"This is so unfair," responded Mercedes. "No one even let me defend myself!"

"Are you serious? I can't believe you did this," accused Giselle.

"But I didn't do it," hissed Mercedes.

"The proof was in your bag and you still smell like cotton candy," declared Evangeline. "I never thought you would cheat to win."

Giselle was too upset to let Mercedes respond. "Why do you care so much about winning? To be some superstar model? You already have GEM Sisters."

"Because I was going to quit GEM Sisters when I won," shouted Mercedes back.

"Quit?" said Giselle in a shocked voice.

"How could you leave us?" accused Evangeline as tears formed in her eyes. "We're a group. We're sisters."

Mercedes tried to think of the words to explain, but all she could focus on was the hurt in her sister's faces.

"Come on Evangeline. Let's go sit somewhere else," said Giselle.

Evangeline stood up to switch seats. "You're my best friend Mercedes. But, right now I feel like I don't even know you."

***

The sun was setting as the bus rolled into the Totally Tiffany parking lot. Everyone but Mercedes was excited to be back. The runway show was only a few hours away.

Doorman Stan greeted the girls with a tense smile. Inside the lobby, Tiffany had already told the parents what had happened.

Tiffany stood near a table that held Mercedes' spa bag and all of the guilty items. There were Jasmine's teal shoes, the cotton candy lotion, and the bottle of green dye.

The parents gasped when Ivy entered the front door.

"Your hair! Ivy, your beautiful blonde hair!" screamed Ivy's mom. She ran to her daughter in a panic. "What has that little monster done to you?"

Ivy's mom ran her fingers through the green hair, hoping it wasn't real. Over and over she lifted up the dark green locks and let them fall. She was in complete shock.

"This is a nightmare!" screamed Ivy's mother, turning to Tiffany for support.

"We can fix this," said Tiffany in a comforting voice. "I've already made a call to get a blonde wig for Ivy to wear tonight. Tomorrow we can have it dyed back to normal."

Before Ivy's mom could respond, Mrs. Harris burst through the front door.

"I was taking a nap at my hotel, but I got here as soon as I could," explained Mrs. Harris. "What's this emergency meeting about? Is Jasmine okay?"

She threw her ugly gray purse with rainbow straps onto the table.

SLAM!

The purse knocked Jasmine's shoes onto the ground. Mrs. Harris instantly recognized the teal heels. She looked at the other items on the table and the bag with Mercedes' name on it.

"That's a GEM Sisters' bag. You stole her shoes! I knew it!" shouted Mrs. Harris to Mercedes.

Jasmine stood behind her mom, looking upset. She was glad her mom was there to stand up for her. She had thought Mercedes was her friend.

"I didn't do it," said Mercedes. "Jasmine, I would never—"

"Are we gonna listen to this liar?"

interrupted Mrs. Harris.

Mercedes' mom stepped in. She was confused by her daughter's actions, but she wanted to protect her.

"Parents, please . . . let's remember these girls are only children. They make mistakes, just like us," said GEM Sisters' mom.

"Mistake? Look at my daughter's hair," shouted Ivy's mom. "This was not an accident, she did it on purpose!"

"Alright, quiet down," said Tiffany to the crowd of parents. "Yes, the proof points to Mercedes, but she says she didn't do it. Does anyone have any evidence to show that Mercedes is innocent?"

The room fell silent. No one said anything.

Mercedes gave her sisters an *aren't-you-gonna-help-me* look.

As Sister Detectives they remembered the facts about the case and how Mercedes had lied to them. She was guilty.

Instead, Giselle looked away and Evangeline stared down at her shoes.

"Well then, there it is," said Tiffany. "Mercedes, you are officially banned from this year's competition!"

Mercedes fought hard not to cry. She

didn't want anyone seeing her get emotional, especially her traitor sisters.

"To the rest of you. We have a show to put on!" proclaimed Tiffany to the group. "Let's get beautiful!"

Parents and their daughters rushed back to the green room. There wasn't much time to get glammed and ready for the big event.

Mercedes pleaded once more. "Tiffany please, I *am* the face of Totally Tiffany. This is a huge mistake."

Tiffany pointed to the bag and all the items on the table. "Sorry sweetie. I had high hopes for you, but there's no excuse for such behavior."

Tiffany turned to see Mrs. Harris standing with Ivy's mom and Fiona's father.

"We've all been talking. Seems only fair that we get something for our troubles," Mrs. Harris spoke for the group. "You need to make this right."

Tiffany was caught off guard. "Okay, well how about you all take my personal dressing room? It's large with lots of mirrors and extra lights."

To everyone's surprise, the parents agreed to share. They left with their daughters to move into their new big dressing room.

Dad felt he needed to clear the air with Tiffany. "So, are we fired?"

He wasn't very good with putting things gently.

Mom cut in, "What my husband is trying to say is that we understand if you would like our whole family to leave."

"No, no, no. You may finish filming tonight. And Giselle and Evangeline can still walk in the show," explained Tiffany. "I'm not going to punish the whole family because of one person's actions."

Tiffany motioned for Doorman Stan to come over.

"Please keep an eye on Mercedes. I want her to remain in the lobby until the show is over," ordered Tiffany.

"You got it Ms. Tiffany," replied Stan with a tip of his hat. "What about this stuff on the table?"

Before she could answer, Tiffany's son Mason interrupted.

"Mom sorry, but people need you," said Mason. "The show is only an hour and a half away. People keep asking me questions that I don't have answers to."

Without a word, Tiffany dashed out of the

room.

Mason glanced at Giselle as he ran off, but she was too busy to notice.

"We're disappointed," Mom told Mercedes. "You've been caught. It could be much worse. So stay put and we'll come get you after the show. Understand?"

Mercedes wanted to defend herself, but she knew it was too late for that. Without her sisters on her side, there was no way her parents would listen.

"No more mischief!" ordered Dad.

Mom and Dad hurried off after Tiffany with their cameras. They still had a job to do.

A quiet stillness filled the lobby. The sisters stood in awkward silence.

"You said nothing!" said Mercedes, finally confronting them.

"What were we supposed to say?" answered Giselle.

"I can't believe you didn't stick up for me. It was so embarrassing!" whined Mercedes.

"We can't be on your side when you're guilty," declared Evangeline.

"Okay fine, let's say I did do it. All of it. Would that be so bad?" said Mercedes. "I wanted to win. I deserve it more than anyone else here!"

"Of course it's bad. It's all bad!" replied Evangeline. "You made Jasmine cry and hurt everyone."

"If you thought I was guilty, you should have talked to me first. We're sisters!" yelled Mercedes.

"Apparently, we're only *sisters* until you get a modeling deal and leave us forever," said Giselle in a rude voice.

Mercedes sighed. "You guys don't understand. You don't care about modeling the way I do. I love fashion, I love getting glammed, and I really love the runway."

"And we supported your dream. Neither of us really cared about winning this contest. We both hoped that you would win," explained Evangeline. "But not like this."

"I didn't do it!" shouted Mercedes. "Ya know what? Maybe I should quit the Sister Detectives too since you both stink at solving cases."

"Fine. Leave Sister Detectives. Go be a *star!* We don't need you," said Giselle.

Mercedes glared at her sister. "Great idea. Not only will I go solo and be super famous, but I'm also gonna take over the Sister Detectives all by myself. I'll solve my own case, prove that

I'm innocent, and look amazing while I do it. Later, dead weights!"

Mercedes found a chair in the lobby. She popped in her earbuds and started watching online videos.

Evangeline was usually the peacemaker, but she was finding it difficult not to take sides.

Giselle was so angry she was turning red. Why couldn't Mercedes ever admit when she was wrong? If Mercedes would just be honest, then they could work together to fix it.

Evangeline didn't know what to say. Maybe Mercedes was telling the truth? Then again, Mercedes lied all the time so how could she tell for sure?

Evangeline knew one thing for certain. If Mercedes was going to be stubborn, then so would Giselle.

"C'mon Evangeline, let's leave the liar," said Giselle.

The sisters loved solving cases together, but now it was over. The Sister Detectives were done forever.

Mercedes said nothing.

Evangeline didn't want to go without hugging her sister goodbye. But, Mercedes didn't even look up when Evangeline put a comforting hand on her shoulder.

Mercedes hid the tears forming in her eyes by staring at her phone.

Evangeline watched the phone screen as Mercedes flipped through different social media accounts. She clicked on video after video of her catfight at the spa. Several contestants had filmed the fight and posted it online.

"Let's go!" ordered Giselle.

All of a sudden Evangeline noticed something. She grabbed the phone out of Mercedes' hands.

"Hey!" screeched Mercedes. "Give it back."

Evangeline ignored her. She quickly scrolled and paused the video. She pointed to the screen.

"Mercedes isn't lying and this video proves it!"

CHAPTER 8

"Watch carefully!" said Evangeline, slowly scrolling through the video.

On the screen, the sisters saw the fight from the spa earlier that day. They watched as Ivy pushed Mercedes and her eyes popped in shock. Evangeline paused the video and giggled.

"Are you making fun of me or helping?" asked Mercedes.

"I'm sorry, your face just looks so funny," chuckled Evangeline.

Giselle joined in. "It's true. You look like you just smelled rotten fish."

"More like fish farts!" laughed Evangeline.

"This is not the time for jokes," ordered Mercedes.

"Sorry," said Evangeline. "Okay, look at the lockers behind Ivy. Do you see that?"

Mercedes and Giselle squinted to see what Evangeline was pointing to on the screen.

"It's a grey blob with bright rainbow straps. So what?" asked Mercedes.

"It's Mrs. Harris' purse. The one she brought to runway practice today," Evangeline reminded her sisters. "She was bragging on her new special design."

"So?" her sisters said at the same time.

"So, it proves Mrs. Harris was at the spa," explained Evangeline. "I think she did all of it. The green hair, the lotion fall, the stolen shoes, the smoothie dress, and probably lots of other stuff we don't even know about."

"You think it was Mrs. Harris? You think she framed me and put those things in my bag?" realized Mercedes.

"Hmm. Even if that's true, the purse at the spa doesn't prove anything," said Giselle. "Jasmine could have borrowed it."

"No. Jasmine didn't have that big, goofy purse on the bus. I would have noticed," said Mercedes. "You're right Evangeline. It *is* Mrs. Harris!"

"Wait, wait, wait! Even if Mrs. Harris was at the spa, that doesn't prove she made Ivy's hair green," explained Giselle.

"Get your proof later. We need to tell Tiffany right now. I've got a runway to walk," ordered Mercedes.

"Hold up! I'm confused. Why would Jasmine's mom do those horrible things?" asked Giselle.

For Mercedes, the answer was easy. "Because she wants Jasmine to win. That's why."

To find out if Evangeline was right, the Sister Detectives had to discuss the clues. Giselle made a list on her phone of what they knew so far.

Mrs. Harris had told Tiffany she was late for the parent meeting because she was sleeping at the hotel. Since the purse was at the spa, she definitely lied. But lying was not enough to prove that she was guilty.

Evangeline pointed out that Mrs. Harris was always nearby when bad things happened. At practice today, she sat in the front row. She could have easily poured lotion on the runway. Not to mention Mrs. Harris's purse was one of a kind, so it had to be hers.

Giselle still wasn't convinced. Why would Mrs. Harris make her own daughter cry by ruining her dress with a smoothie or stealing her shoes? It didn't make sense.

Evangeline didn't have an answer for Giselle's question. But in her mind she knew she was right. Mrs. Harris was guilty. No other person made sense.

"We can't just say she's guilty. We have to show Tiffany facts and evidence," explained Giselle.

The sisters peered out the lobby windows and saw cars arriving. Doorman Stan opened the front door and greeted the guests. Everyone entered wearing fancy dresses and their best suits.

"It's hopeless. The show is basically starting," whined Mercedes. "You should go get ready. You both still have a chance to win."

"Hello? We're sisters!" said Evangeline. "We care about *you*, not winning. You deserve to walk the runway and live your dream."

Giselle and Evangeline wrapped their arms around Mercedes and hugged her tightly.

"Listen, if Mrs. Harris is the bad guy then there has to be proof. We just have to find it," encouraged Giselle.

"But she put all of the evidence in Mercedes' bag," said Evangeline.

"There could still be other clues Mrs. Harris

forgot," realized Giselle. "Like maybe gloves she used for the green hair dye, or a bill proving she bought it."

"Her purse!" squealed Mercedes. "That's where girls keep all their stuff."

"She keeps that purse closer to her than her own daughter," said Evangeline. "That's gonna be tough!"

"Maybe Jasmine would help?" said Mercedes hopefully.

"Fat chance," said Giselle. "She's more likely to become Ivy's BFF then to trust you again."

"To her, you're like a creepy snake. No, worse. A rotting worm. No, a teeny tiny piece of bacteria that lives on the rotting worm," said Evangeline.

"Enough! I get it. She hates me," groaned Mercedes.

"Mrs. Harris will not get away with this. We're gonna find that purse and you are gonna walk the runway," commanded Giselle.

"Thanks for believing me big sis," said Mercedes. "I wish I could help, but I'm stuck in this big dumb lobby."

"I know! We'll video chat. Then it will feel like you're with us," said Giselle.

She handed Mercedes her phone. Giselle

told her to use one phone for video chatting and one phone to look for clues on social media. They were going to need all the proof they could get.

"But stay out of my camera roll and don't text anyone," warned Giselle.

"No promises," teased Mercedes. "JK."

An announcement came over the doorman's radio saying, "The runway show starts in one hour. I repeat, one hour."

Giselle's face got very serious as she said, "Come on Sister Detectives. We have one hour to prove Mercedes isn't guilty. Let's do this!"

***

Backstage was buzzing with girls and parents rushing around. Some girls were getting makeup and hairstyles done, while others practiced their runway walk. All of the girls wore bright pink robes, waiting to put on their original Tiffany designs.

Giselle and Evangeline knew they had to avoid getting ready for as long as possible. They put on pink robes to help them blend in. Giselle found a clipboard with a list of what order the girls were walking in the show.

First on the list was Fiona, then Ivy, and then Jasmine. At the bottom of the lineup were GEM Sisters, but Mercedes' name was crossed out.

"Looks like Tiffany had planned on having Mercedes close out the show," said Giselle.

"Guess Mrs. Harris was wrong," said Evangeline. "Best is last."

"Well luckily being last gives us more time to look for clues," said Giselle.

The sisters snuck around the room turning their backs every time one of Tiffany's workers walked by. They scurried their way over to a door by a long hallway. They tried to peek inside the small window on the door when it flew open! A worker quickly exited the room.

"And my Jasmine needs ice cold water! Not this warm water bottle you brought me," shouted Mrs. Harris at the worker.

"Ivy needs the melon picked out of her fruit bowl. She hates melon," complained Ivy's mother.

"And we thought *Mercedes* was a diva," joked Evangeline.

Luckily, the worker left the door open which made it easier to see inside. The sisters sat on the ground against the wall. They hid behind a couple of folding chairs.

Inside the small room they saw Mrs. Harris holding her grey purse with rainbow straps.

"She's got a death grip on that bag. How in the world are we going to look inside?" asked Evangeline.

"We've got to find a way to make her put it down so we can grab it," said Giselle as she closed her eyes to think of a plan.

Evangeline interrupted her thoughts by opening the video chat on her phone.

"Grumpy Slothicorn to Drama Llama. Come in. Do you hear me? Over," asked Evangeline, acting like her phone was a walkie talkie.

"Shush! No code names!" ordered Giselle.

"Too late Captain Smarty Pants. Over," giggled Mercedes on the screen.

"Where are you? Over," asked Evangeline.

"Um, newsflash. Still in the totally boring lobby. Over," replied Mercedes.

"We're mega bored here too. Over," said Evangeline.

"Can you guys be serious for once?" begged Giselle.

"Do I have any boogers in my nose? Over," asked Mercedes as she smooshed her face against the phone screen.

Mercedes and Evangeline giggled then stopped. They could feel Giselle's angry eyes.

"Did you find any clues on social media yet?" asked Giselle.

"I've literally checked over a hundred posts and still nothing. Mrs. Harris has like, no social media followers. Her most popular picture is doing laundry with the caption, *Sock Washing Saturday!*" groaned Mercedes.

"It's not going great here either," said Giselle. "We can see Mrs. Harris holding her purse, but there's no way to get it."

Giselle pointed to another door at the back of the dressing room. Evangeline turned the phone screen to show Mercedes.

They couldn't tell if it was a closet door or another way inside the room. The Sister Detectives decided to sneak around the back hallway to check it out.

"Hey!" came a booming voice from behind them. "What are you doing? The runway is the other direction."

Giselle and Evangeline froze. They slowly turned to see Mason standing behind them.

"The runway? Sure, that's where we're going. I can't wait to watch you strut your stuff on the runway," blurted Giselle.

Mason looked confused. Giselle kept rambling.

"I mean no, we're walking the runway. Duh! You're taking the runway pictures. Not pictures of the runway, pictures of me. I mean us!"

Evangeline stared at Giselle, who could not stop embarrassing herself.

"Well, I'm definitely going to be taking pictures of you," replied Mason as he locked eyes with Giselle.

Mercedes cleared her throat. "We don't have time for your crush problems," she said sternly over the phone.

Giselle's face blushed bright red at Mercedes' comment.

"Oh hey!" said Mason. "Sorry you're out of the show. I personally enjoyed your evil pranks, but my mom not so much. I've seen girls play dirty to win, but you are the master."

Mason did a little bow with prayer hands to Mercedes, but she didn't find it funny. He then turned and held Giselle's hand.

"I know you gotta get ready for the show, but just promise me you'll never change. I think you're perfect just as you are," said Mason.

Giselle froze. Her heart was racing so fast she didn't even notice that Mason had let go of her hand and was walking away.

Evangeline shouted, "Hey Mason! That other door in your mom's personal dressing room. Is it a closet or is it another way in?"

"It's a closet!" he shouted back.

"Drat! Well that's a dead end," said Evangeline.

Giselle's possible boyfriend drama would have to wait. Right now the Sister Detectives still had a case to solve, and they were running out of time. The sisters hurried back down the hallway discussing a new plan when—

"Gotcha!" said a worker wearing a headset. "I've been looking for you two everywhere. It's time for the glam squad."

Evangeline started to make an excuse, but the worker didn't listen. She seated them both in front of large mirrors with big bright lights. The glam squad put black capes over their robes and started brushing and curling the sister's hair.

"You guys are getting glammed? That's so unfair," whined Mercedes on the video chat.

Getting her hair and makeup done was not Evangeline's favorite. She never understood why Mercedes liked it so much. All of the pulling and poking was more annoying to her than fun.

"I would gladly trade places," complained Evangeline.

Out of the corner of her eye Giselle noticed the door to Tiffany's dressing room was still open. With the parents talking loudly, it was easy to hear what was happening inside.

"Jasmine! You gotta turn left, not right," ordered Mrs. Harris.

"Chin up," yelled Fiona's dad.

"Move your hips," shrieked Ivy's mom.

Giselle whispered to her sisters, "They must be practicing their runway walks."

"Watch it loser!" yelled Ivy.

"Sorry. I didn't mean to run into you. I keep forgetting to turn left," apologized Jasmine.

Ivy mocked her, "You are seriously so terrible. I'm glad you're after me because when the crowd sees you, they won't be able to stop laughing."

"Watch yourself!" warned Mrs. Harris to Ivy.

"It's the truth, just sayin'," announced Ivy.

"Jasmine, I'm gonna go see what's taking so long with your ice water. You keep practicing. I'll be right back," said Mrs. Harris.

"Target is on the move," whispered Giselle.

"Huh?" replied her sisters.

"The package is out the door."

"What?"

"Mrs. Harris!" said Giselle annoyed. "She's leaving the room with her purse."

"Oh. Why didn't you just say that?" asked Evangeline. "Let's go!"

"Wait!" said a woman from the glam squad. "Your hair is only half curled!"

"We'll be back," lied Giselle. "I gotta use the restroom ASAP or it's going to be a disaster."

Evangeline jumped out of her chair and followed Giselle. "Um, yeah, she needs my help. Ya know, sister support."

"What's happening?" asked Mercedes on the phone.

"We're following Mrs. Harris," replied Evangeline. "She's going to the other side of the stage."

"Shh! She's going to hear us," ordered Giselle.

The Sister Detectives quietly followed Mrs. Harris. They stayed hidden in the dark shadows behind the stage. Workers in black clothes busily ran back and forth. Thankfully, the sisters were still wearing the glam squad's black capes, so it was easier to blend in.

"Where did she go?" worried Giselle.

Mrs. Harris had disappeared like a ghost.

Evangeline carefully peeked from behind the curtains. Out front the DJ blasted music which made her want to dance. Mom and Dad were setting up cameras and lights. Her eyes searched the crowd. There was no sign of Mrs. Harris.

Giselle noticed another door to the side of the stage. The lights were turned off and it was dark inside. A beam of light appeared in the window on the door.

"Look!" whispered Giselle. "Someone's in there with a flashlight. I can see a bunch of clothing racks."

"I want to see. Turn the phone," ordered Mercedes in a loud voice.

"Hold on. We'll call you back," said Giselle as she ended the call.

Giselle knew they needed to act fast. "I think Mrs. Harris is inside. I don't know what she's up to, but it can't be good."

Evangeline and Giselle quickly formed a plan. They snuck into the room together. Gently, they closed the door without making a sound. Inside the room, they crawled on the floor using their black capes to hide in the darkness.

The room was filled with racks and racks of clothes. This was where Tiffany kept the final outfits until it was time to go on stage. She wanted the models to wait until the last minute to change so there were fewer wrinkles on the runway.

Giselle crept closer to the flashlight. She saw Jasmine's mom standing next to a rack of clothes. Mrs. Harris was holding a small bottle in her hand. She shook the bottle all over the clothes like a salt shaker.

Evangeline saw it too. This was the proof they needed. Quietly, she held up her phone and opened the camera. She zoomed in and pressed the record button.

BUZZ! BUZZ! BUZZ!

Mrs. Harris turned her head toward the sound.

On the phone screen Mercedes was calling to video chat. Quickly, Evangeline pressed the button to end the call. It was too late. Mrs. Harris had heard the sound and was slowly creeping toward her.

Evangeline ducked down and hurriedly crawled under a clothing rack. She didn't have time to look for Giselle. She knew they were in danger. She pulled the black cape over her whole body like a blanket to hide.

Evangeline was so scared she could hear her own heartbeat. Mrs. Harris' footsteps grew louder the closer she got. Sneakily, Evangeline sent a text message and then powered down her phone so it wouldn't buzz again.

Back in the lobby, Mercedes' phone beeped a text message alert. There was only one word on the screen.

HELP!

CHAPTER 9

Mercedes was in a panic. She had sent several text messages with no response. She tried to video chat over and over, but Evangeline didn't answer.

Maybe she doesn't have WiFi, Mercedes thought.

There was still one thing she hadn't tried. A phone call. She and her sisters preferred to video chat, but she knew this was how old people used their phones. She dialed. The phone rang. Then she heard a voice answer.

"Hi. It's Evangeline."

"OMG! Thank goodness you're alive," started Mercedes.

"If it's Monday, scream your message. And if it's Tuesday, text me cause I'm eating tacos. But if it's Wednesday, tell me the name of your favorite stuffed animal . . ."

Mercedes rolled her eyes and set the phone down. It was Evangeline's voicemail and clearly it was going to take a while. After a long breath, she picked up the phone again.

"What's that? It's Saturday? Then what are you waiting for? Leave me a message. And extra points if you're wearing your underwear backwards today. If you don't know, then check. I'll wait."

BEEP!

"I'm not sure if you'll hear this, but I'm coming to save you!"

Mercedes ended the call. She didn't know how she was going to save her sisters, but she had to try.

She glanced over at Doorman Stan. Almost everyone had arrived so he was busy playing games on his phone. Mercedes thought about sneaking away, but that could get her in even more trouble.

Without her sisters she felt helpless. Giselle and Evangeline were the planners. Mercedes' job was basically to do whatever she wanted. Or at least she was pretty sure that was her job as a Sister Detective.

She closed her eyes. She imagined her sisters tied to a chair while Mrs. Harris mocked them with her evil laugh.

"Worrying won't solve this," decided Mercedes. "I need help. Okay phone, you've never let me down before. Tell me what to do!"

The phone did nothing.

That's it! she thought.

Mercedes kissed her phone and shoved it into her back pocket. She picked up Giselle's phone and texted as fast as she could.

MEET ME IN THE LOBBY. COME QUICK! I NEED HELP.

Moments later Mason came zipping around the corner.

"Mercedes?" said Mason, surprised. "Where's Giselle? She said she needs me."

"She does. I can't explain, but you gotta trust me," begged Mercedes.

"Cool. I'm in."

She had prepared this whole speech about why he should trust her, but Mason didn't need to hear it. If Giselle was in trouble then he was ready to help.

"Can you sneak me backstage? There's a room behind the curtains. I think my sisters are trapped in there," worried Mercedes.

"I know exactly where that is. That's the room they store all the new clothes in before the show starts. Let's go!" replied Mason, starting to run off.

"Wait! I'm not supposed to leave," whispered Mercedes. "Could you lie to Doorman Stan for me? If you don't want to I underst—"

"Stan my man," interrupted Mason. "My mom wants Mercedes to wait backstage during the show. Cool?"

"Whatever," Stan replied without looking up from his phone game.

Mercedes was in awe of Mason's lying abilities. He wasn't as good as her, but he definitely had "the gift."

Mason took off his faded sweatshirt revealing a wrinkled t-shirt underneath. "Here," said Mason, handing Mercedes his hoodie and camera. "Put this on and hold up the camera to cover your face."

Mercedes shrieked as she placed the old, gross, stinky sweatshirt over her adorable outfit. Ew! Using a costume to hide was a good idea, but this plan had turned into something totally gross and embarrassing.

For a moment she wished she hadn't contacted Mason. Then she thought of her sisters in trouble. She had to help them, even if it meant becoming a fashion nightmare. After she saved their lives, they were going to owe her big time.

"If people think you're a photographer, they'll pretty much let you go anywhere," explained Mason, motioning her to follow him. "Now c'mon!"

Mason led her down the busy hallway. As they got closer to the stage there were more and more people. Everyone was working hard to start the show. Mercedes kept lifting and lowering her camera, playing her part as the photographer.

"Through here!" said Mason, leading Mercedes backstage. "Is this the room?"

Mercedes nodded. She recognized the same dark doorway that she had seen earlier on the video chat. They both walked in and flipped on the light.

EMPTY!

There were no clothing racks and worst of all, no sisters!

"Where are the clothes?" worried Mercedes.

Mason responded, "Oh my mom always hides the outfits so no one can guess her show theme. She gets kinda crazy about it. Since the show starts in ten minutes the clothing racks will be in the dressing rooms now."

"No time to lose!" yelled Mercedes, freaking out.

"Whoa! I wanna help find Giselle but like, that's a girls' dressing room. My mom has a strict no-boys policy," said Mason. "I'd wish you luck, but you're wearing my lucky sweatshirt, so you don't need it. Tell Giselle to text me when you find her."

"I will," shouted Mercedes, handing him his camera back.

As she ran off, Mason was about to tell Mercedes to stay out of trouble. He figured that probably wasn't going to happen.

There were only ten minutes 'til showtime so Mercedes had to act fast. It was easy to snoop with everyone running wild with last-minute fixes. Her sisters were nowhere. She was starting to worry.

Mercedes watched as Fiona, Ivy, and Jasmine got their final hair touch-ups. She noticed Mrs. Harris wasn't with Jasmine like the other parents. A worker came up to the group and handed a fashion mask to each of the girls.

"I'm excited to tell you this year's runway theme. It's a Masquerade Ball," squealed the worker.

"I don't do sports. And I'm not holding a ball," replied Ivy.

"It's not about sports. It's a fun costume party where everyone wears a mask to hide who they are," explained the worker.

"I like the idea of hiding Ivy's face," said Fiona with a smirk.

The worker continued, "Time to put on your outfits. If you need help with how to hold the mask, please let me know."

"Are the girls judged on how they hold the mask?" Fiona's dad spoke gruffly. "The runway walk is fifty percent of their score and you just gave her this mask! There's no time to practice."

The dad's question stirred up the other parents in the room. They were each concerned the mask was going to hurt their daughters' chances of winning.

The argument allowed Mercedes to sneak by the group and into the row of small dressing rooms. This was the same place Jasmine had her smoothie dress disaster! Maybe this was where Mrs. Harris was holding her sisters. Quietly, she listened outside the doors, but heard nothing.

Mercedes pulled out her phone. No new

messages. Once again, she called Evangeline.

"Hi. It's Evangeline. If it's Monday, scream your message. And if it's Tuesday . . ."

She hung up the phone and groaned. "It's hopeless. I'm never going to find them."

Mercedes leaned against the wall. She couldn't see it, but a hand slowly reached out from behind the dressing room door. Before she could scream, Mercedes was yanked inside. She was face to face with . . . her sisters?!?

"You guys scared me to death!" complained Mercedes.

"SHHH!"

"We don't know where Mrs. Harris is, so we've been hiding in here," explained Giselle.

"But more importantly, what in the world are you wearing?" giggled Evangeline.

"Ugh! Don't even! Why didn't you answer my messages?" asked Mercedes. "I texted you like a zillion times. I even called and left a message like an old person!"

Evangeline remembered her silly voicemail message and giggled.

"Seriously, what happened?" said Mercedes. "I was so worried."

"It was horrifying!" said Evangeline. "First we went into that scary dark room. And then we saw Mrs. Harris. So, we crept along the floor to get a closer look."

"She was holding a small flashlight. It was really hard to see, but it looked like she was pouring sand from a salt shaker on the outfits. It was weird," added Giselle.

"I tried to film and catch her in the act," continued Evangeline, "but right when I pressed record, you tried to video chat us!"

"Oops," said Mercedes. "Sorry about that."

"We ducked down but Mrs. Harris had already heard the phone buzz. Luckily, we had our black fashion capes on. We covered ourselves like a blanket and hid," said Giselle.

Evangeline whispered in a spooky voice, "Mrs. Harris was standing right over me. I could hear her breathing. She bent down to pull off my cape. I knew we were done for."

"But then the lights switched on and she scurried away like a cockroach. The workers came in, so we stayed put. We rode out of there on the bottom of the clothing racks," said Giselle.

"So Mrs. Harris didn't see you? That's good. But we still don't have any proof," replied Mercedes. "We should give up. The show starts in five minutes."

"We can't quit," begged Evangeline. "We need to figure out what she's planning. That mean mama is clearly up to no good."

Giselle agreed, "Yeah and we still don't know what the sandy stuff is that she sprinkled over the outfits."

Evangeline's and Giselle's runway outfits were hung up on the dressing room wall. Mercedes leaned in close to see what looked like small specs of sandy dirt on the clothes. Giselle explained that she needed more than a few specs to figure out what it was.

"I've been trying to perform a science test on the dirt specs, but I need a safe way to collect them into a pile," explained Giselle.

"That's easy!" said Mercedes.

In a flash, Mercedes took off Evangeline's black cape and laid it on the floor. Then she grabbed one of the outfits off the wall. She shook the dress. Small specs fell like snow onto the cape.

"Ah Splart!" sneezed Evangeline.

"Stop!" ordered Giselle. "Quick, cover your mouth and nose."

"Tah Dah! One pile of weird dirt just like you ordered," said Mercedes, proud of herself.

Giselle put her hand over Mercedes' mouth.

She explained that now those dust specs were in the air and could be harmful. In science class, she always wore goggles, gloves, and a face mask to be extra safe.

"Uh, you could have said that before," complained Mercedes.

"Well it's done now," said Giselle. "Hmm, I need a piece of paper."

Evangeline looked around the room. She found the runway show lineup taped to the door and said, "Here ya go."

Giselle wished she had her science tools from home. Slowly she scooped the dust pile onto the paper, being careful not to touch it. Mercedes turned on her phone flashlight so she could see better. Close up, it looked more like powdered sugar than dirt. The color was light brown with speckles of red.

The sisters all wondered what it could be. Giselle sniffed the powder slightly. She was careful to not get it in her nose, but gently breathed in the smell. It had a slight odor, almost like flowers. She thought hard and remembered her grandmother's rose bushes.

One summer, she had helped her grandmother plant roses in front of her house. Giselle explained how the powder had that same faint smell of roses. Weird. Maybe Mrs. Harris was helping to freshen up the designs?

"What I'm about to do is not safe," warned Giselle. "So if I swell up like a balloon or pass out, call a doctor! I hate to do this, but without proper tools, what choice do I have?"

"You're so brave," said Evangeline. "Or dumb. Either way, I admire your courage."

Giselle had looked at the powder and smelled it, but now she was going to lick it. Slowly she stuck out her tongue.

"Don't!" shouted Mercedes. "I know what it is. I'll tell you, but you have to promise not to get mad."

"Why do I feel like that's gonna be impossible?" answered Giselle.

"It's itching powder," said Mercedes. "It's made from roses."

"How could you possibly know that?" asked Giselle.

"That's not important," lied Mercedes. "So now that we know what it is, what should we do?"

"Not so fast. How can you tell it's itching powder?" asked Giselle.

"Well . . . remember last summer when we had that sleepover in the backyard?" said

Mercedes slowly.

"You mean that time when we itched like crazy all night long!" screamed Giselle.

"Yeah. I thought it would be funny to prank you and pour some itching powder in your sleeping bags."

"That was you!" yelled both of her sisters together.

"You told me you saw fleas in my sleeping bag!" whined Evangeline. "I threw away my favorite stuffed animal because I thought it had fleas too."

"You got so mad I couldn't tell the truth. But hey, we can laugh about it now. Right?" said Mercedes with a nervous giggle.

Her sisters weren't laughing. Their eyes pierced Mercedes for what seemed like forever, but was actually only a few seconds.

FWEET! FWEET!

A worker blew a loud whistle to get everyone's attention. Evangeline peeked her head outside the door to see what was going on.

"Ladies, it's time to line up. The show is starting!" said the excited worker.

The Sister Detectives huddled together. They were out of time, but they still had to solve the mystery. They had discovered it was itching powder, but they did not know why Mrs. Harris had sprinkled it on the clothes.

"Why make everyone itchy?" questioned Evangeline.

"That's it!" realized Giselle. "The runway walk counts for half of your score. So, whoever has the best runway walk wins."

"Umm, are you going to tell us something we don't know?" asked Mercedes annoyed.

Giselle continued, "What if Mrs. Harris put itching powder on everyone's outfits but Jasmine's? Every other girl will be walking like they have ants in their pants. Jasmine will be the only contestant with a perfect runway walk."

"Which means Jasmine will win," said Mercedes.

"That's so evil," shrieked Evangeline. "We have to stop her. Jasmine is my friend, but we can't let her cheater mom win."

"There's still no proof she did this," explained Giselle.

Mercedes looked at the outfits hung up on the wall. Her eyes darted to the pile of itching powder.

"Where did she put all of the bottles?" asked Mercedes. "Itching powder is expensive and it comes in little clear bottles that only hold two tablespoons. It would take at least 40 bottles of itching powder to cover all the outfits."

"Her ugly purse!" said Giselle and Evangeline at the same time.

"It's the only place that the workers wouldn't find the empty bottles. She can't risk throwing them away because her plan might get discovered," said Giselle.

"Mercedes you're a genius," squealed Evangeline.

"I know. It's hard being this smart and pretty, but someone has to do it," replied Mercedes.

FWEET! FWEET!

"All parents follow me! We have your seats ready in the front row," shouted the worker.

The Sister Detectives peeked out from behind the door. They saw Mrs. Harris in line with the other parents.

"I'm sick of this. I'm going to grab her purse and dump it out in front of everybody," hissed Mercedes angrily.

Giselle pulled her back into the room.

"No, you can't! If anyone sees you, we're all in trouble!" begged Giselle.

"She's gone now anyway," said Evangeline,

peeking out the door.

"So, what then? Mrs. Harris gets away with it?" asked Mercedes angrily. "This is so unfair!"

"We figured out the mystery, but we still can't stop her," said Giselle with a sigh. "I'm sorry."

"It's okay. I know you tried your best," said Mercedes.

Giselle gave Mercedes a loving, big sister hug. They had lost. Mrs. Harris had won.

"I really wanted to walk the runway," Mercedes said sadly.

"If you can't walk, then we won't either, right Evangeline?" asked Giselle.

"Wrong!" replied Evangeline. "We're all going to walk the runway together!"

Evangeline grabbed a fancy party mask and held it to her face.

"No one in the crowd will know it's us!" said Evangeline with a smile. "It's time to unmask the real troublemaker behind these runway rumors."

CHAPTER 10

"Welcome sweeties to my annual Totally Tiffany runway show!" squealed Tiffany.

The crowd cheered and whistled excitedly. Tiffany wore a dazzling, long red gown. She sparkled in the bright spotlight. The DJ played an upbeat song that matched the rhythm of the dancing disco lights.

Mom and Dad stood on opposite sides of the stage filming. They spoke to each other in their headset microphones.

"Get a wide shot of the crowd and I'll focus on close ups," said Mom in her director's voice.

"I don't know about you, but this music is making me want to shake my booty!" joked Dad.

Mom didn't answer. She wanted to get a perfect shot of the first girl walking onto the runway. This was a live show, so there was only one chance to get it right.

"This year is my best collection yet," said Tiffany. "And the girls modeling for you tonight make my clothes look fabulous."

Tiffany started explaining the rules for her model contest to the eager crowd.

Meanwhile, backstage, things were not as calm. Workers ran back and forth making sure each girl looked perfect. Some of the girls standing in line started to complain that their outfits felt itchy.

Still in the dressing room, the Sister Detectives were planning just how they would expose Mrs. Harris. They couldn't wear their itchy clothes, so Evangeline worked quickly to create new designs worthy of the runway.

Luckily, this weekend Evangeline had already been creating one-of-a-kind outfits for her very own fashion collection. She dug through her special suitcase of odd items. Quickly, she sewed and pinned decorations onto her sisters' new outfits.

"What's this stuffed animal for?" asked Mercedes.

"Oh, you'll see," replied Evangeline. "Now be still. I don't want to poke you with the needle."

Mercedes held her breath as Evangeline

sewed a cute pink puppy stuffed animal onto her sparkly skirt.

"Perfect!" squealed Evangeline.

She turned Mercedes to face the mirror.

"Wow! This outfit is amazing," said Mercedes surprised. "At first I was like 'Eeek!' but now I see you really have a gift."

"I've learned that fashion is about taking risks," explained Evangeline. "Now Giselle, come here so I can pin these cute donut erasers to your shirt."

Back out front, the crowd roared as Tiffany ended her speech.

"Now, are you ready to see the theme for this year's show?" shouted Tiffany.

Cheers broke out all over the room.

Tiffany spoke louder, "I can't hear you. I said, are you ready?"

The crowd was fired up even more than before.

Tiffany took a deep breath. "I give you, my Masquerade Ball!"

The curtains pulled back to reveal Fiona standing in the spotlight with her adorable freckled face. She wore a black velvet dress with a blue sweater and posed with her mask. The crowd clapped and snapped pictures.

Fiona, however, was feeling very itchy. She had worn lots of horrible fabrics for modeling shoots before. Many had made her sweat or want to scratch, but this outfit was the worst by far. She forced back her urge to itch and started walking.

Tiffany saw Fiona's strong entrance on the runway, and turned to face the crowd.

"Fiona is wearing a bold design that says 'I am Tiffany.' I feel beautiful because I am beautifully dressed," said Tiffany, proud of her outfit.

Fiona's long legs walked boldly with large steps. She pushed back the tickling feeling on her skin that said it wanted to be scratched. Each step seemed to make the feeling worse.

She made it halfway down the runway before she gave in. Her skin needed to be scratched. Fiona couldn't resist any longer. She tried to hide itching her shoulder as she posed.

By the time Fiona reached the end of the runway, she was at a breaking point. She ripped off her mask and started using it to scratch her back. Once she started, she couldn't stop. Each scratch felt so good.

Dad talked to Mom over the headset mic, "Are you seeing this?"

"What is going on? I don't remember this from practice earlier," replied Mom as she zoomed her camera closer on Fiona.

Tiffany hid her confused face. She had no idea what Fiona was doing, but she needed to keep the show on track. She acted like everything was fine.

"These clothes make her so happy she wants to dance," lied Tiffany.

Fiona's dad shouted at her from the front row, "What are you doing? Be still. You're ruining your chance to win!"

She tried to listen and pose, but she couldn't. Instead, Fiona ripped off her cute blue sweater and tossed it to the ground. She screamed as she ran backstage. "Aaaaaahhhhh!"

Tiffany could see the crowd was puzzled, so she came up with another lie. "I am girl power. Hear me roar! Am I right? ROAR!"

The curtains closed and the crowd awkwardly clapped. Off to the side of the runway Mason snapped pictures. He had no idea what was going on, but he was pretty sure Mercedes was behind it. To him, the show was an amusing mess and he couldn't help but laugh.

Backstage, Ivy didn't waste her chance to insult Fiona. "Wow! That was horrid. Thanks for making it so easy for me to win."

Fiona was scratching so much she didn't even respond. She ran past Jasmine and Ivy in line. Jasmine thought about going after her new friend, but she wasn't supposed to leave her spot.

Out front, Tiffany forced a smile and motioned her workers to open the curtains, "Next we have Ivy-Tastic!"

Ivy stood in the spotlight holding her dog Percy. She wore a hot pink polka dot romper. She and her dog wore matching white masks. The crowd clapped at how adorable they were.

"Everyone will be jealous of you and your furry friend in this snazzy outfit. It's perfect for school and for hanging at the mall," explained Tiffany.

Ivy felt the itchy burning immediately. She tried to use her other foot to itch her leg as she walked. She almost tripped, but played it cool. Percy started scratching because he was itchy too.

"You can walk your dog in style," continued Tiffany.

Ivy did everything to force herself to walk

and not itch, but she couldn't take it any longer. She stopped in the middle of the runway. Everyone wondered what she was doing.

She set Percy on the ground then got down on all fours. She started itching like a dog and crawling. Ivy looked like a dog with fleas.

The crowd gasped.

"Or I guess you can act like a dog," said Tiffany with a nervous giggle. "Thank you Ivy for that delightful puppy walk."

Everyone started laughing. Ivy picked up Percy and sprinted off the runway.

"Get me out of these horrible clothes!" demanded Ivy as she ran backstage.

"Looks like my bold designs are causing the girls to make some bold runway walk choices," said Tiffany. "How about that dog impression? I need to create a dog fashion line. Am I right?"

The crowd stared back blankly. Tiffany had lost them. They were confused and disappointed with this fashion-show-fail.

Dad whispered into his headset mic, "I'm no fashion expert, but this show seems—"

"Embarrassing?" filled in Mom. "This is NOT how a runway show is supposed to go."

"Do you think Mercedes had anything to do with this?" asked Dad.

"I sure hope not," worried Mom.

Mom and Dad wanted to go backstage, but they had to stay put and keep filming the show. If Mercedes was behind this, she was going to be in big trouble.

Backstage Ivy yelled at everyone, even Percy. "Why am I so itchy? Who did this? You're all going to be sorry. I'm telling everyone on social media how awful Tiffany's clothes are!"

Still in the dressing room, Giselle watched as Ivy threw a fit.

"This whole show is falling apart. Time to go," Giselle ordered her sisters.

Evangeline wished she had more time to put the final touches on her designs. It was her first fashion show after all. But right now being a detective was more important. The sisters grabbed their masks and headed to the stage.

The itchy models had all the workers running around in a panic, so it was easy to blend in.

"Whoa! This is a hot mess," noticed Mercedes.

"Stay close," ordered Giselle. "If anyone spots Mercedes we're done for."

They crept around a corner that led to backstage. A worker was holding a clipboard.

He instantly realized they shouldn't be there.

"Hey! It's not your turn. And what are you wearing?" asked the worker.

"Listen!" urged Giselle. "Tiffany needs you to get everything on this list. These items will help the girls stop itching."

The worker read the list Giselle had made. On it were things like ice packs, special lotion, and oatmeal. Thanks to Mercedes' sleeping bag prank, Giselle knew how to get the models some relief.

"How did you talk to Tiffany when she's hosting the show?" asked the worker doubtfully.

Giselle froze trying to think of what to say. She wasn't the best at lying.

"Mason told us. He's not allowed back here so he gave us the message," lied Mercedes. "He said his mom is super angry. You'd better go if you want to keep your job."

The worker ran off with the list in hand.

"Still the master," bragged Mercedes, proud of her lie.

The Sister Detectives hid behind the curtains and slowly took a peek. Out front the crowd was going wild for Jasmine's turn on the runway. She smiled and posed as she twirled.

"Look! She's not itching," said Giselle. "That

means we are totally right about Mrs. Harris'
plan to help Jasmine win."

"But we still don't know if Jasmine is part
of her mom's evil plan or not," Evangeline
reminded her sisters. "Jasmine could only be
pretending to be nice."

Mercedes watched Mrs. Harris smiling
smugly by the front of the runway. She held her
purse on her lap and hollered the loudest.

"I'm going to love snatching that purse and
showing everyone she's guilty," said Mercedes.
"Then we'll see who's smiling."

Jasmine started her walk back down the
runway. Giselle wanted her sisters to go over
the plan one more time. They only had one
chance to do it right.

"Remember, we need to work together so
no one recognizes you Mercedes," explained
Giselle. When we get to the front, Evangeline
and I will pose to distract the crowd so you can
grab her purse. Okay?"

Giselle waited for her sisters to answer, but
Mercedes was gone!

Just then, Jasmine entered backstage,
proud of herself. A worker greeted her and said
she'd done an amazing job. Then they called out
the name of the next girl to walk.

"She's already on stage," Jasmine explained to the worker. "She was there when I was walking off."

"Mercedes!" Giselle and Evangeline whispered at the same time. They peered from behind the curtains. Sure enough Mercedes was already posing on the runway.

"There goes my plan," whined Giselle.

Evangeline and Giselle jumped out from behind the curtains and joined Mercedes on stage. The crowd went wild, cheering with their every step. The sisters walked together to the beat of the music, moving their shoulders and flipping their hair.

"Next up is a fashion first that will knock your socks off!" said Tiffany, looking down at the schedule. "These Tiffany original designs are . . ."

Her voice trailed off as she looked up. The three girls in masks had on wild outfits that were definitely not Totally Tiffany. They weren't even a little bit Tiffany.

Evangeline's designs were full of neon colors, crazy textures, and wild patterns inspired by her sketchbook.

Where did these outfits come from? wondered Tiffany. She smiled bigger even though inside she was about to lose it. This show was officially a disaster.

The Sister Detectives in disguise swung their hips and strutted their stuff down the runway. The crowd was loving the girls' energy as much as Evangeline's designs!

Evangeline nodded to the people and started clapping to the music. She got them clapping over their heads first right and then left. Giselle did some freestyle dancing while people grooved to the beat.

"These outfits are a surprise to my collection," lied Tiffany.

Behind the camera, Mom could see the panic in Tiffany's face. "Oh no! It's the girls. What are they doing?" she asked Dad.

"It's probably safe to say we aren't going to get paid for this job," Dad replied in his headset mic.

Whatever happened, Mom and Dad knew there was no way to fix it now. The damage was already done.

Mercedes was having so much fun. This was her moment. This was why she dreamed of being a model. The lights, music, and crowd was such a rush. She loved the way it made her feel and never wanted it to end.

Giselle saw Mason on the side of the runway. She posed and smiled just for him. Secretly, she hoped he would ask her to go on a date after the show.

However, standing behind Mason, was Giselle's mom and she did not look happy.

"Mom knows! Repeat. Mom knows and she's got crazy eyes," Giselle whispered to her sisters.

"Mercedes grab the purse," urged Evangeline. "We're running out of time!"

The Sister Detectives still had a job to do. Mercedes went into action. She danced at the edge of the runway, sneakily looking for a way to take Mrs. Harris' bag.

Sadly, the stage was much higher than she had remembered. She leaned all the way over and made a swipe for the purse. Nope. It couldn't be reached. There was no way this was gonna work.

"Keep your masks on and follow my lead," whispered Mercedes to her sisters.

Giselle did not like the sound of that, but she didn't have time to argue.

Mercedes walked over to where Tiffany was standing and grabbed the mic.

"Everyone give it up for Tiffany and this wonderful show," shouted Mercedes.

The people answered with glee.

"These outfits are the surprise part of Tiffany's collection. The designs were inspired by a special someone in the crowd," continued Mercedes.

Tiffany stood frozen with her mouth open. She didn't know what was happening.

"Can we get a spotlight on the front row?" asked Mercedes. "Everyone clap for Mrs. Harris and her one-of-a-kind purses. Come on up!"

Evangeline and Giselle supported Mercedes and got the crowd clapping. Mrs. Harris sat shocked for just a moment, before happily bolting onstage.

"Let's see you strut the runway with your fabulous purse," encouraged Mercedes.

Mrs. Harris posed and smiled. Before Tiffany could grab the microphone, Mercedes turned and motioned for Mrs. Harris to come over.

Giselle and Evangeline didn't know what the plan was, and they weren't exactly sure Mercedes knew either.

Faces peeked out from behind the curtains. Workers and models wanted to see what was going on. They knew this was not part of the show. Jasmine saw her mom onstage and was the most confused.

"Come here and tell us about yourself Mrs. Harris," said Mercedes, still wearing her mask.

"Well, my daughter is Jasmine," said Mrs. Harris. "She's the beautiful girl that totally nailed her runway walk. And she—"

Mercedes interrupted with fast interview questions.

"Mrs. Harris, what inspires your designs?"

"My daughter."

"What color is your favorite purse?"

"Red."

"Do you hope your daughter wins the contest?"

"Of course."

"Did you put itching powder on all of the girls' dresses?"

"Yes. I mean NO!"

The music stopped suddenly and the crowd went silent.

The Sister Detectives pulled off their masks.

"Ah ha!" said Mercedes who had grabbed a hold of the purse.

"Give that back you crook!" proclaimed Mrs. Harris. "Now you're stealing purses!"

"I'll give it back, after I show everyone that I'm innocent," said Mercedes. "Tiffany, it was Mrs. Harris who poured the smoothie on Jasmine's dress and stole her shoes. She also put lotion on the runway to make Fiona trip. She even snuck into the spa to dye Ivy's hair green."

"That was you!" shouted Mrs. Harris.

"No, it wasn't," said Giselle, sticking up for her sister.

"It's true. She put that stuff in Mercedes' bag to make her look guilty," added Evangeline.

"Of course they're gonna lie for each other, they're sisters," explained Mrs. Harris. "Now give me back my purse. Me and Jasmine are leaving!"

"Okay, fine," said Mercedes, acting like she was going to give it back. "Oops!"

Mercedes purposely dumped the purse onto the runway.

Dozens of empty clear bottles spilled everywhere. Tiffany picked one up and read the label:

ITCHING POWDER

CHAPTER 11

The contestants flooded onstage to get a closer look. Mrs. Harris wanted to lie to the crowd, but everyone stared back with shocked, angry eyes. She put her head down in shame. She was caught.

"I did it," said Mrs. Harris with her hands covering her face.

"Ha! See, I knew I was innocent!" yelled Mercedes as she did a happy dance. "Woo!!!"

Giselle reached out and touched Mercedes on the arm. "Not now," she whispered.

"Explain yourself," demanded Tiffany, handing Mrs. Harris the microphone.

Mrs. Harris stammered, "Tiffany, I'm so sorry. I never meant to hurt anybody. It's just that, well, my little girl has never won a contest and probably never will."

Jasmine felt so many emotions as she

listened. Anger. Embarrassment. Sadness.
She felt terrible about Fiona's ankle. She felt
even worse seeing her new friends all itchy and
miserable.

Mrs. Harris was now sobbing. "Jasmine was
never gonna win unless I made it happen. To
me, she's the prettiest girl in the world. But
other people don't see her that way. They think
she isn't tall enough, or skinny enough. She's
got a big heart, but Jasmine doesn't look like
the girls that win these contests."

Tiffany frowned. She did not want people
feeling sorry for Mrs. Harris. What she did
was wrong. Jasmine's mom had hurt so many
people and ruined the weekend.

"Don't ya see? Nobody cared about Jasmine
until her dress got ruined. She was being
ignored until I made people feel bad for her,"
continued Mrs. Harris. "But it's all my fault.
I did this, not her. Please, please, please don't
punish my daughter."

"I need you to leave," said Tiffany, motioning
her workers to take Mrs. Harris away.

Everyone glared at Mrs. Harris as she
started walking backstage.

"Mama, how could you?" asked Jasmine.

"I'm so sorry, baby," Mrs. Harris replied,

fighting back her tears. "I just wanted everyone to see you like I do."

Jasmine put a comforting hand on her mom's shoulder. She looked at the furious crowd and walked to the front of the runway. Slowly, she picked up the microphone.

"What my mom did was wrong, but she's also right. I don't look like the girls you see on commercials or in magazines. I knew I wasn't going to win, but guess what? I don't need to win to feel like a winner."

Jasmine took a deep breath. She looked to her friends for support.

"I believe that all of us girls are beautiful in our own way," continued Jasmine. "Whether you have freckles, or brown skin, or you're tall or short, or if you have thin hair or poofy hair. You can be skinny or curvy because there isn't one kind of pretty. Being different is what makes us special."

The models standing on the runway felt as if Jasmine was speaking to their hearts. Some of the girls put their arms around each other. Mercedes looked down at the brown skin on her arms and smiled. Fiona grinned at Jasmine, thinking of her freckles.

Jasmine continued, "And the clothes we

wear don't make us beautiful. Our outfits only help to express who we are. Every girl should be made to feel pretty just being herself. I'm lucky. My mom has always made me feel that way. I hope you girls know that you're all winners and that you're perfect just being you."

Jasmine handed the microphone to Tiffany. "I'm very sorry for what my mom did. We'll leave now."

Tiffany watched the runway models nod and support Jasmine as she turned from the crowd. GEM Sisters pulled her in for a goodbye hug.

"I'm really sorry about what happened to you," said Jasmine to Mercedes.

"Thanks," said Mercedes. "What you just did was really brave."

"You're an amazing girl with a huge heart," encouraged Giselle.

"Promise you'll keep shining bright," added Evangeline.

Jasmine couldn't hold back her tears any longer. Fiona came up and put her arm around her friend. They both walked backstage.

Tiffany didn't know what to do. Mason gave his mom an encouraging smile. She looked to all the models still standing on the runway.

Tiffany cleared her throat, then spoke into

the mic. "I'm very sorry, but I'm ending the fashion show without choosing a winner. I hope you understand."

The crowd groaned. Contestants lowered their heads, upset and confused.

"However, all is not lost," Tiffany continued. "Models, I know you're leaving town tomorrow. Before you go, please join me in the lobby at 8:00 am sharp. Everyone is invited. There will be a big announcement! And I mean big!"

***

The next day, people started gathering in the Totally Tiffany lobby. Everyone arrived early hoping to be the first to find out the big announcement. Doorman Stan greeted people as they walked in. Unlike last night, no one was wearing fancy clothes.

The lobby was unusually quiet. There was no music. It felt bare and lifeless. Even the giant posters of models hung up around the lobby were covered with black curtains.

Anxious reporters stood with cameras and microphones. They had lots of questions, including if Tiffany was going to pick a winner. Mom and Dad also had cameras setup and ready to film.

The GEM Sisters stood with the other contestants, waiting for answers. Evangeline munched on a plate of chocolate donut holes and cut up melon.

"How can you eat at a time like this?" asked Mercedes.

"I think it's rude not to eat," said Evangeline as she took another bite. "They don't put out food for people to look at it."

Fiona entered the lobby and waved when she spotted GEM Sisters. They could tell Fiona's dad was still grumpy from last night's failure.

Ivy and her mom glared at everyone. They were both still angry about her green hair.

"Glad your friend isn't here to cause more damage," Ivy said to Fiona. "You know, Jasmine was right by the way. Cheating was the only way she was gonna win!"

"You'd be lucky to have a friend like Jasmine," answered Fiona. "I feel sorry for you. You're only mean because you don't have any real friends."

With a flip of her hair, Fiona walked away.

Ivy shouted after her, "I don't need friends. I have followers!"

The girls looked around the room, but there was no sign of Jasmine or Mrs. Harris.

At exactly 8:00 am Tiffany walked up to the podium on the small stage. She wore a plain white t-shirt and jeans rather than her usual high fashion look. Sitting next to her was Mason, wearing a different wrinkly sweatshirt.

"Sweeties! Thank you for coming," said Tiffany in her happy, excited voice. "I am about to tell you the biggest announcement ever in the history of Totally Tiffany."

The crowd started to chatter. Everyone was guessing what she was going to say. Dad zoomed in for a close-up of Tiffany, and Mom filmed the crowd.

"This year's contest has had more challenges than any other," said Tiffany. "I've decided it's time to change how I do things."

Mom filmed the worried faces in the crowd. Many people wondered if Tiffany was canceling the prize. Or perhaps, there would be no winner this year.

"First, I want to thank my team who stayed up with me all night to make these changes," continued Tiffany. "Let's hear it for my amazing crew."

The workers took a bow and the crowd

whistled their praises.

DING!

Giselle got a text message and quickly silenced her phone. Sneakily, she looked at her screen. It was from Mason.

HEY BEAUTIFUL. CAN'T WAIT FOR YOU TO SEE WHAT I'VE BEEN WORKING ON.

Giselle locked eyes with Mason on stage. He smiled and gave her a wink.

Through his camera lens, Dad also noticed the wink. He looked over at Giselle who was blushing. Dad decided to wait, but he was definitely going to have a talk with Mason after the announcement.

Tiffany quieted the crowd. "I've always said fashion makes beauty. But I was wrong. My Totally Tiffany clothes don't make girls beautiful. Look at these ladies. They're already beautiful. Each one is so different and special."

In Dad's close-up shot, he could see that Tiffany was getting teary-eyed. She took a deep breath, then continued.

"There is no one perfect girl we should all try to look like. From now on, I will only make clothes for girls to express their true selves. Which is why I'm changing my company name from Totally Tiffany to Totally You!"

A neon sign behind Tiffany lit up with the new company name "Totally You." The crowd perked up and cheered.

"And I have chosen all of the contestants to be the new faces of Totally You," Tiffany proudly shouted. "You're all winners!"

Around the room, Tiffany's workers pulled down the curtains on the giant posters. The models gasped. Every girl from the contest was featured. Seeing their picture on the wall made some of them start crying happy tears.

Mom zoomed in on smile after smile of the girls in the crowd. They were all so honored and excited. Everyone that is, except for Ivy who was bubbling with rage.

"What? No! You can't change the rules in the middle of a contest!" shouted Ivy. "I'm supposed to win. I'm the most beautiful and perfect!"

Mercedes quickly pulled out her phone and started to film. "GEMS we found out that we all won the contest! Ivy, I heard a rumor that you're upset about sharing first place with everyone. Is that true?"

Ivy scowled at Mercedes. She was so angry, that for the first time she showed her true self in front of the camera.

"Forget all of you losers. I'm the only real

winner. Mom, we're leaving!" screamed Ivy as she stormed out of the room.

Mercedes continued filming. "I guess the rumor was true and Ivy-Tastic won't be joining us. What a bummer. That's okay, the rest of us will still have lots of fun without her. Byyyeee!"

The contestants couldn't stop staring at their huge posters. The longer they looked, the more real it felt. Giselle noticed Mercedes, lost in thought, staring at her own giant picture.

"Mercedes, I'm sorry you weren't the only winner. I know this contest meant a lot to you," said Giselle.

"Are you kidding?" Mercedes said, snapping out of her daydream. "This is so much better. Now, every girl in the world gets to celebrate how amazing they are. We helped make that happen!"

"Once again, Sister Detectives saved the day," said Evangeline, posing like a superhero.

"Thanks for sticking by me," said Mercedes in a serious tone. "I can't believe I thought about leaving GEM Sisters. I hope you can forgive me."

"We're sisters," said Giselle. "We'll always have each other's backs."

Giselle and Evangeline squeezed Mercedes

tight in a group hug.

"We should charge Tiffany for solving the case," realized Mercedes. "I'm sure she'd be glad to pay us a few hundred dollars. Don'tcha think?"

Giselle and Evangeline both rolled their eyes and chanted together, "Oh, Mercedes!"

The Sister Detectives didn't solve cases for the money. They did it to help people. Still, hearing Mercedes asking to get paid meant that she was back to her old self. That made them both happy.

Tiffany tapped on the microphone to get the crowd's attention. "Everyone! Just a few more announcements before we start the party. Can GEM Sisters please come to the stage?"

Dad whispered into his headset mic, "Um, what's this all about?"

"I have no idea. Maybe the girls are still in trouble," Mom replied.

"Yesterday, these sisters wore runway designs that weren't mine," said Tiffany in a hurt voice.

Mercedes whispered into Evangeline's ear. "If we get in trouble, I'm totally blaming you."

"I've since learned that those designs came from this talented young lady," said Tiffany, pointing to Evangeline. "Your clothes are young, fun, bold, and fresh."

Evangeline couldn't stop smiling.

"Will you do an exclusive GEM Sisters' fashion line with my new company Evangeline?"

"Darling, I'd be delighted!" Evangeline said in her silly French voice.

Tiffany paused for a moment. Where had she heard that accent before?

Mercedes pushed her way to the microphone and said, "My own clothing line? Yes! OMG! It should be pink for sure and glitter of course and—"

She suddenly stopped. Mercedes took a step back and gently pushed Evangeline toward the microphone. It was her little sister's turn to shine.

"As GEM Sisters, we believe fashion is an awesome way to express yourself. We would love to encourage girls with our very own fashion line," said Evangeline.

Their model friends in the crowd whistled and clapped wildly.

"And if you like my ideas so far, don't worry. There are plenty more up here," Evangeline said, pointing to her head. "Like cheese pants, donut bracelets, and avocado hats."

Instantly the crowd went from cheering to confused.

"The point is, yes!" said Evangeline, hugging her sisters as she spoke. "But only if we do it together."

Mom and Dad were relieved that it was good news. They beamed with pride as they filmed their daughters walking off stage.

Back in the crowd, Evangeline was glowing. That was, until she saw Jasmine's big poster on the wall. "I wish Jasmine could be here to see that she won too."

Giselle turned to Fiona. "Have you talked to her since yesterday?"

"No," Fiona replied. "I've sent tons of texts, but she hasn't answered any of them."

"Her mom may be crazy, but Jasmine is amazing. She's the one who made all this happen," said Mercedes.

Fiona agreed. "Jasmine helped me see that my freckles make me special. I don't hide them anymore. I'm proud to show them off!"

"Your freckles are seriously goals," said Giselle.

"Everyone, please quiet down," said Tiffany. "Now, just one more announcement before we start the party. And for this surprise, I need the person who helped me see that I was wrong about fashion and beauty."

Jasmine walked out onto the stage. The crowd went wild.

"Actually, I think you should tell them the surprise," Tiffany said to Jasmine.

"I'm excited to be the leader of the new Totally You club for girls. This group is all about being positive and building each other up," said Jasmine. "We are going to encourage girls all over the world to love themselves and celebrate what makes them special."

Jasmine pulled out her phone and held it high to take a selfie with the crowd.

"I want everyone here to be in our first post," explained Jasmine. "Smile big and say 'Be your own kind of beautiful!'"

CLICK!

"Now, everyone go follow our new page and like this picture," ordered Tiffany. "Okay DJ, let's start the party!"

Music blasted. Parents danced. Daughters were embarrassed. Fiona's dad joined a crowd of parents thanking Tiffany for her speech.

Jasmine walked up to GEM Sisters and Fiona. The friends all hugged and told Jasmine how proud they were. They were so happy to be together again.

"Mercedes and Fiona, if it's okay with you, my mom has something she'd like to say," said Jasmine.

Mrs. Harris entered the girls' circle. She was carrying yet another handmade purse. It was a peach color with big silver letters that spelled out "Proud Mama."

"I am so very sorry, girls. There's no excuse for what I did," said Mrs. Harris. "It's never okay to hurt people. Even if it's for good reasons. Right is right and wrong is wrong. I'm sorry for doing you wrong."

"Honestly, I was super angry. And it definitely hurt," said Mercedes slowly. "But we have to forgive each other when we make mistakes. My sisters taught me that. I forgive you."

"Same for me. I wouldn't have a BFF if Jasmine hadn't forgiven me," said Fiona.

"I'm gonna work extra hard to make it up to you girls. Jasmine has lots of ideas she needs help with," said Mrs. Harris. "We want every girl in the club to feel special."

"Let us know if GEM Sisters can help," offered Giselle.

Out of nowhere, Evangeline shouted, "This

is my favorite song! Form a conga line!"

Mercedes was first to line up behind her sister, followed by all the models. Evangeline led the group with silly dance moves as they giggled and danced around the lobby.

Out of the corner of her eye, Giselle spotted Mason across the room. She broke away from the group and went over to him.

"I like the picture you took of me," said Giselle, looking up at her poster. "All of the girls look amazing. You're really talented."

Mason smiled at Giselle's praise, "I was hoping I could get a selfie to remember you by."

He held out his phone and Giselle leaned in close. They both smiled.

CLICK!

Right when Mason pressed the button he turned and kissed Giselle on the cheek.

Giselle's heart started racing. "Well, I think it's only fair that I get a picture so I can remember you too."

Giselle held out her phone. She puckered up her lips and closed her eyes. Slowly she leaned toward Mason . . .

"Smile!" said Dad, popping up right between them ruining their kiss. "I think we got it. Don't you agree Mason?"

From across the room, her sisters saw that Giselle needed help. They broke from the conga line and hurried over. Sadly, by the time they got there, Dad had already scared Mason away.

Mom joined the family. "I'm still wondering about yesterday. How exactly did Mercedes get on the runway? She was supposed to stay in the lobby."

Uh oh, thought the girls. *Mom hasn't forgotten.*

"Well, we knew Mercedes wasn't really guilty," said Giselle, trying to think of an excuse.

"You're right mom," interrupted Mercedes. "Right is right and wrong is wrong. I should've stayed in the lobby. Maybe you should ground me when we get home?"

"Well, sounds like you learned your lesson," said Dad, confused. He was used to Mercedes arguing when she got caught. "I guess we can skip you getting in trouble just this once."

The girls could see Mom still had more questions. Thankfully, Tiffany had asked their parents to start filming again.

"Maybe I should tell the truth more often?" said Mercedes. She thought about it for a moment. "Nah! That doesn't feel right."

They giggled and joined their friends on the dance floor.

Today all the girls in the contest learned that what made them different, made them special. What the Sister Detectives didn't know was that the next mystery was going to be their biggest adventure yet!

About The Authors

MéLisa and Ryun
(aka Mama GEM
and Papa GEM)
have been partners
in art and life for
over 20 years.
Together the
authors share a
passion for creating
funny children and
family entertain-
ment for all ages to
enjoy. When they're
not penning books,
they're writing
comedy sketches
and funny videos
with their daughters, GEM Sisters, on their popular
YouTube channel and website www.gemsisters.com.

Their inspiration for writing books came from
encouraging their daughters to love reading as much
as they did growing up. After an enthusiastic response
from their first book, the authors have now penned
multiple series with the wish that young readers
everywhere will put down their small screens and
open up their imagination. MéLisa and Ryun hope
that their books will add a little laughter to your day.
Current series include "Spy Pets" and "Sister Detectives."

MORE
Funny Mysteries
By The Authors

For Readers Ages 6-9
Buy Online Wherever Books Are Sold!

Support Sister Detectives!

Leave A Book Review

Tell Your Friends About The Book

Share on Social Media

www.gemsisters.com

Meet GEM Sisters!
Join the GEM Sisters Club. It's free!
Get updates about a book signing near you!

Made in the USA
Middletown, DE
31 July 2020